PUCK PROPOSAL

THE WILCOX WOMBATS
BOOK 3

DELANCEY STEWART

PROLOGUE

JULIUS RAMON (AKA ICE CLEANING
MACHINE DRIVER)

Like all things, cleaning the ice in a hockey rink takes years to perfect. Sure, the machine does most of the work, but the guidance and precision of the operator creates the final result.

Hockey, of course, is similar. You don't just throw on a pair of skates and find yourself on a team like the Wombats. My nephew knew that. And while it was hard to see Mizzoni retire, it was the right time for him. Time to allow others to rise up and take his place.

John Samuels is a worthy replacement.

If only John himself could see it.

CHAPTER 1
JOHN

MEET HANK. IT'S HIS HOUSE.

It was bordering on darkness when I got home from the gym, nearly exhausted. June was the off season, which gave me a few months to build myself up, to hone my skills and my body. A few months to deserve the opportunity that had come my way late last season when Stephano Mizzoni left the Wombats, making me the youngest starting goalie in the FHL.

Living up to the expectations the team had for me would be tough, and more than that, I didn't want to let Mizzoni down. His approval--his friendship--was hard won, and I respected him. A lot. Still, the expectations I was most worried about were my own.

I'd worked my ass off for this chance.

And now, like my dad loved to point out, it would be pretty damned easy for me to blow it.

I guided the sleek black truck I'd just acquired into the garage. It almost didn't fit, thanks to the truck being huge and the garage being relatively tiny. But it didn't matter.

They were both mine, outright. Everything I had was mine, and I'd earned it all myself.

The engine purred to a stop and I shut it off, letting myself sit for a bit, doing my best to live in the moment, to appreciate where I was. What I had achieved.

But fuck, Dad's voice was always in my ear, and I wondered, at what point would it all be enough for him? Or at what point would I stop caring what he thought? I wanted to make the All Star team this year, to show him that I had support—even if it wasn't from him.

I hopped out and grabbed my gear, blowing out a long breath and doing my best to clear my head as I stepped inside the house and hit the button for the garage door.

I went weeks without falling back into the pit of self-recrimination that Dad had helped me dig as a kid. But then I'd talk to him, and he'd find ways to push me back in.

"Your brother's getting married," Dad had announced this morning when I'd called him to check in. "Can you believe it? He built a brokerage and a house, and now he's gonna build a family." The pride in Dad's voice was unmistakable and, as always, it leveled me. When my father spoke to TJ, did he sound this proud about me?

I already knew the answer.

TJ was the miracle kid. The baby who was delivered blue and still, but who magically came back to life against all odds. He was the star athlete, the star student, and being three years older than me meant everything he achieved marked the first time a Samuels kid ever did anything. Leaving me always trailing behind.

"He told me, Dad." I'd already talked to TJ, who was

thankfully less enthusiastic about reciting all of his many incredible attributes than my father was. Teej and I were friends. Always had been. It wasn't his fault he'd been born first. Or that our mother had died giving birth to me.

That was just the luck of the draw.

Hank came prowling around the corner as I stepped into the entryway between the garage and the laundry room, his sleek gray head leading the long athletic body. He dropped to sit directly in front of me and tilted his head to the side, looking up at me with deep green eyes and letting out a single long *mmm-ow*.

"Hey buddy." I dropped my gear and leaned down to scoop up the cat, who looked up into my face and put his front paws on my neck. "How was your day?"

Hank was more dog than cat, but he was also self-sufficient when I traveled with the team for games or left for long hours to run the annual camp I'd built for kids. He was a perfect companion for me—always proud of me, always happy to see me. He'd arrived on my doorstep as soon as I'd bought this house, and I suspected he might have lived here before and been abandoned. I'd asked around the neighborhood and taken him to be scanned for a chip, but no one had been able to help me locate his family, and Hank seemed pretty convinced he lived with me.

So I let him.

It was nice coming home at the end of the day, having someone eager to spend time with me, willing to listen.

Even if that someone was a cat. When you'd scrambled for every bit of attention you'd ever managed to receive, you weren't picky about where it came from.

I showered and cooked, settling myself next to Hank on the couch at the end of the day and flipping on some old tape to review to keep me company. Sometimes I went out with a few of the guys from the team—Mario and Van usually. We were the youngest, and I guess we felt most comfortable together. Joining the Wombats was a lot to wrap your head around, and stepping in to stand next to some of the best players in the league was tough. Those of us who were new looked out for one another, helped each other.

But those guys had families to visit, girlfriends to spend time with.

I was just glad I had Hank, even though it was kind of hard to get used to his favorite spot to watch television, which was behind me on the top of the couch, his paws kneading my head.

As the video from last season's last game rolled, I picked up my phone and called Mizzoni. There was one play in the last period I hated watching. I knew I'd let a stupid one past me, and I still wasn't sure how I'd do it differently. But Mizzoni would know. It was three hours earlier in California, so I knew he'd still be up.

"Hey, Samuels," he said.

"Mizzoni. How are you?"

"Honestly?" he asked, a smile in his voice. "I've never been better. How are things in Wilcox? How's the team?"

"Pretty good," I said. "Just trying to stay in shape, work out some kinks before next season."

"I saw the last few games, John. There aren't a lot of

kinks. You're a great goalie. And you know how hard that is for me to say."

"I appreciate it. The words, and how hard it is for you to say," I laughed. "I just don't want to take the chance for granted."

"Yeah, well, there's something to be said for time off too."

I turned myself on the couch, moving my head out of Hank's attentive grip. He let out a meow, and hopped down into my lap, shooting me a green-eyed glare before curling into a circle and tucking his head. "I think I need to use the time to get better. I just don't want to blow things."

"Most players take at least a month off the skates. Your body needs the rest."

I blew out a breath. "I know it sounds kind of superstitious ..." I began.

"Oh here we go. Okay, what is it?"

"I just have this feeling if I let myself relax, everything will vanish. Like if I spend a day off skates, if I just let my guard down, it's all going to be gone when I try to step back on the ice."

"That's kinda fucked up. The talent is in you, not in some magical practice you're undertaking, which, by the way, will also set you up for an injury if you're not careful. Take it from someone who's been there."

"Yeah...I do appreciate your advice..."

"But you're not gonna take it."

"I'll try. I will. In fact, I wanted to see if I could get a little more of it."

"Oh yeah?"

"Did you watch the home game last season against the Storm Chasers? I let one through in the third period?"

"Ohh, yeah, that was a rough one."

"I was just watching it again, and I still can't see how—"

"John."

"Yeah?" I scrubbed a hand over my face. Mizzoni's voice had taken on the 'tough love' quality and I sensed I wasn't going to like what he had to say.

"Let it rest. We all let one in now and then."

"Yeah, but if I figure out how to do better, then—"

"How many times have you rewatched that play?"

"A lot."

"Then you already know. Man, you've gotta take it easier on yourself. Tomorrow. No skating." Mizzoni's voice had become lower, a growl, and I remembered how intimidating he'd been when we'd first met. Of course, back then, he'd been worried I was going to take his position on the team.

His worries had been well founded, as it turned out.

"I'll just do a light day. I'm not going to lift tomorrow. I've got stuff to do for camp anyway—a lot more kids coming this year."

"Well that's good," he said. "But the workouts..." I could almost hear Mizzoni's disapproval in his breath, though he said nothing else. His silence made me feel like I should explain myself. Like if I just told him how important it was that I hang onto this opportunity, that I prove I'm worthy of it, he'd understand. But he was already talking.

"Hey, man, I have to go. Hillary's got this thing tonight I promised I'd go to."

"Yeah, totally. Sorry to keep you."

"No, I'm glad you called. Just... John?"

"Yeah?"

"Take it easy on yourself, okay? You're fucking talented. That's not going to vanish overnight."

"Yeah, okay. Thanks. Tell Hillary hi for me."

"I will."

We hung up and I let Mizzoni's words seep in around the anxiety I couldn't seem to shake. I knew he was right— I'd gotten this far. But I could do more. Better. And that wouldn't happen if I let my guard down. When I got where I was going, I'd rest.

Hank raised his head and narrowed his eyes at me, as if he could read my thoughts and didn't approve any more than my mentor did.

"Go back to sleep," I told him. Hank let out a little meow and then dropped his head again.

On the screen, the clash between the Wombats and the Storm Chasers unfolded, and I tensed, anticipating the goal I had let slip past me in the dwindling moments of the third period. I tapped the remote, reducing the playback speed to dissect my error in agonizing detail. The play developed: their center, a fucking wizard with puck control, seized a breakout pass and dashed across the blue line, evading our defenseman with a slick deke. He barreled into the offensive zone, eyes flicking between me and his winger on the rush, keeping our defense guessing.

As he approached the faceoff circle, he feinted towards the boards, luring Simpson to overcommit. With a swift cut back to the center, he created just enough space for a clear shot. I was anchored in the crease, my stance ready. But he unleashed a low, sizzling wrist shot, and I knew in that second I'd made a critical error. I'd shifted too far left, and there was no time to correct. I cringed as I watched myself thrust my right leg pad out, but it was too late. The puck slid through the narrow gap of the five hole.

The red light blazed behind me, a glaring reminder of my lapse. The sting of that moment, the sharp pang of failure, surged through me all over again. Not enough. In that moment—In so many moments—I'm just not fucking enough.

CHAPTER 2

JOEY

BEAUTY SLEEP IS CRITICAL

"You look like a fairy princess." My cousin Geneva drew her little hands up under her chin and sighed, staring up at me on the pedestal at the dressmaker's shop as I forced myself to stand still for last-minute alterations.

"Thank you, honey," I told her, forcing a smile her way.

She was just a kid. She didn't know any better.

The truth was that I was about the furthest thing from a fairy princess there was. I was a woman in a ridiculous dress having very dark thoughts.

"Ouch!" A pin lanced the sensitive skin beneath my arm.

"Sorry, Joey. I just don't understand how you've managed to lose so much weight. You're gonna have to share your secrets." Maggie, my mother's seamstress gave me a wink of her false lashes and then jabbed another pin into the fabric, pulling the bodice of my wedding gown tighter across my chest.

I had lost weight.

The pathetic thing was that I wasn't trying to lose weight at all. Which was annoying, considering how many failed diets lay strewn across the path behind me. It turns out all you need to drop pounds is to agree to a wedding you shouldn't have and then let your mother push you around like you're twelve again. Worked for me!

"You look perfect," my mother said, stepping into the room with her phone still in her hand. "And don't worry about a thing. I've ensured the catering is all finalized and all you have to do after this afternoon's rehearsal is show up and put on this dress." My mother narrowed her gaze at Maggie. "Which Maggie will absolutely have delivered to the dressing room no later than eight o'clock tomorrow morning."

"Absolutely!" Maggie answered.

"I tried my dress on again too," Geneva said earnestly, looking up at me with wide blue eyes set deep in her fair skin. "Just to be sure."

"Thanks, sugar," I said, giving her a grateful smile. "You'll be the very best flower girl Peach Blossom Grove has ever seen." I knew Geneva just needed a little approval, but I wanted to tell her that it wasn't my acknowledgment that was important. I might be wearing the dress, but this wedding was one hundred percent the purview of my mother, Adelaide Baxter, and I was pretty sure everyone over age ten knew it.

I was merely a mannequin. An automaton going through the programmed motions of Adelaide's grand design, which was something she'd evidently gotten from the master rulebook of society mothers in the Deep South.

> *Step one: have a daughter*
> *Step two: force her to learn a bunch of manners*
> *and dances before the age of twelve.*
> *Step three: put her in a white dress and introduce*
> *her to society like some craft project you've*
> *been putting the final touches on for the last*
> *seventeen years.*
> *Step four: marry her off to someone who's been*
> *through the exact same program, except on the*
> *side designed for boys.*
> *Step four-A: extra points if that boy is the son of a*
> *wealthy local family.*

I'd let myself be pushed around my whole life, following Mama's plan, and now here we were, on step four, just like that. There was a garish diamond gleaming on my finger, and tomorrow morning, I'd watch the very last shreds of my independence slip away as I agreed to become Mrs. Evan Stratton.

"All done!" Maggie trilled, stepping back to admire her work on the custom gown my mother had commissioned almost a year earlier.

"Wonderful." Mama gave Maggie her approving smile and then waved a hand at me. "All right, Josephine, darling. Let's get you home for a bit of rest. I'm so glad I planned for an early rehearsal dinner. You'll have plenty of time for a full eight hours before you need to put this dress on again."

Because beauty sleep was critical.

As were sunscreen, moisturizing one's feet and cuticles every night before bed, and drinking no less than ten glasses of water daily. Mama's rules were clear and easy to follow. As long as you didn't have any silly ideas about thinking for yourself.

The sun shone down as I helped my mother into the passenger side of the huge silver SUV my daddy had bought for me to take to college. Mama hated it, but Daddy had insisted it was the safest thing he could put me in. I loved it. It was huge and sporty and fast, and exactly the opposite of everything my mother approved of. It was my one rebellion.

We made the short trip from downtown Peach Tree Grove to our house, nestled back on a shady tree-lined street and protected by a white fence running the periphery of the yard.

This was where I'd grown up. And at times, it had been idyllic. Now, though, the straight slats in the white fence felt more like prison bars, and the walls of my mother's perfect home were a cage I'd managed to get locked up in again, despite having escaped once before to college.

I pulled into the driveway, but didn't shut off the engine. My gaze was fixed straight ahead, down the shady drive, dangerous thoughts in my mind. I couldn't seem to shut them off.

"Well, let's go in, Josephine. It's stifling out here." Mama opened her car door and slipped out, then turned back to face me. "Well, honey? Are you coming?"

I shook myself out of the daze, fighting off the thoughts

pushing their way through my mind. Thoughts of escape, of freedom, of terror at what was coming at me in a matter of hours.

"I am. I just remembered I need to go pick up some eye cream. I'm all out."

Mama let out an exasperated noise. "I don't know why you didn't mention that when we were out, darling. You need some time to recharge before tonight."

I nodded. "It won't take long."

Mama sighed and pushed the door shut, and I watched her make her dainty way up into the back door of the house. She meant well. She loved me, I knew that. I was her only child—who could blame her for doting?

But I was also a woman with a degree, a woman with dreams. A woman who'd thought there would be time for adventures and exploration, but who'd also dated a boy from her tiny hometown when they'd struck up a friendship in college, and then come back home engaged to him. I was a woman who'd believed Evan knew my heart, who was sure he understood me.

I was a woman who'd been terribly wrong.

As soon as we'd come home engaged, wheels were set in motion that I felt powerless to stop. Instead of interviews, resumes, and a long engagement, I was suddenly faced with pressure on all sides to marry. Immediately. To host my mother's friends, to meet the executives at the firm Evan was going to inherit from his father, to entertain.

Mama convinced me to move back in with them since I'd just have to move again in a year when Evan and I got married. I should have said no. I should have said no to many things.

I sat in the driveway a moment longer, and the rushing sound inside my head grew louder. Something was coming at me, like a herd of wild horses stampeding in my direction or a freight train loaded with something that would definitely make a mess when it exploded. Like glitter. Or Miracle Whip. And if I didn't act now—right now—I'd be overcome by whatever it was.

I backed the big car out, glancing around the perfect street where I'd grown up, and guided it slowly away.

When I crossed out of Peach Tree Grove's town limits and pushed the accelerator down the open highway headed north, I pulled up Evan's number on my car's Bluetooth, my heart beating hard. I wasn't sure what I was going to say, but he deserved something.

"Hey babe, isn't it bad luck to talk the day before the wedding?" Evan had been making up all kinds of dumb wedding rules for weeks. It had been sort of cute at first. Now it wasn't.

"You're not supposed to see me the day of." My voice shook a little when I spoke, and I tried not to imagine Evan's face, or what it would feel like for him to understand I was running away. From us. From him.

"That's gonna make it hard to say vows, won't it?" There was a chuckle in Evan's voice, and I cringed at the knowledge of what I was about to say to him. The knowledge that it would erase any desire to chuckle. I didn't want to marry Evan. But I wasn't eager to hurt him, either.

"Ev, I think I've made a terrible mistake."

"That's all right, babe. We'll handle it. We're in this together. What's up?"

Dammit, he was always such a good guy. That was what had attracted me to him in the first place. That, and our parents basically arranging this engagement when we were ten. It had taken getting away from their influence, meeting him under new circumstances at college, for me to agree that he was actually a great guy.

But I didn't think he was the right guy. For me.

"No, you don't understand. Evan, I don't think we should get married."

There was a beat of silence, and then another light laugh, less confident. "Wedding day jitters, I guess, huh?"

"No, I don't think so."

"What are you saying, Joey? You can't be serious." Evan's voice got a little higher. "Where are you? Let's talk about this."

"I know the timing is awful, I know it..." My voice rose as tears pressed into my eyes.

"It's not just the timing." Evan made a noise that sounded halfway between desperation and disgust. "Please tell me you're kidding."

"I'm not kidding. Evan, but you have to know it's not you. It's not about you at all. I just... I just realized I can't do this. It isn't what I want."

"That sounds very much about me. Tell me where you are. We'll talk."

"I'm leaving. I'm in the car. I'm halfway to Georgia." I glanced at the signs on the highway. I wasn't even close to

Georgia yet, but I wasn't turning around. Every mile that passed made me more sure I was doing the right thing.

"What?" Evan's voice pitched higher. "Babe, please don't do this. Come back."

"Do you really think getting married is the right thing for you, Evan? Right now? Before you've had a chance to do anything? To see anything?"

"I've got everything I want right here. Joey, I love you. Don't you love me?"

I swallowed back the lump in my throat and blinked away the tears spilling down my cheeks. "I do," I said honestly. "But I don't think I love you in the way people who get married should love each other."

"Love is love, Joey. Come home."

Love is love.

I didn't think that was true.

Didn't love make you want to see the person you were with achieve their dreams? Didn't it make you wish for them everything they wished for themselves?

"I think there are lots of kinds of love, Ev. And you deserve the kind that wants to be your wife. You deserve someone who loves you the way you want to be loved."

"I don't..." Evan, never at a loss for words, seemed to be at a loss for words. "Honey, please."

"I'll call you in a couple days. Please apologize to your parents for me. I really am sorry." My stomach twisted.

"Oh god. Please don't do this." His voice broke.

"Bye, Evan." I hung up, and the tears came for real.

But I wasn't crying over Evan, not really, though I didn't like the idea of hurting him and I knew I had. I was crying with regret for what I knew my parents would go through, for the embarrassment and wasted money, for the enormous cake and the custom dress...

But I was also crying with relief. Because every bit of road that passed beneath my tires was one more inch of freedom. And by the time I really did reach Georgia, I found that I could finally take a deep breath. I could finally start to be me again.

CHAPTER 3
JOHN

I woke up to a gloriously bright sunshiny day, and decided that maybe Mizzoni had a point. Driving myself relentlessly might not be the answer.

And it was only one day. I could stay off skates, maybe even not think about hockey at all, for one whole day.

In the kitchen, I got Hank his wet food as he wound around my ankles, and then glanced at my phone. I had a couple messages from Elliot, the manager my foundation had hired to run the summer camp for kids. Last year, I'd done most of the work myself, but now that Mizzoni was gone and the camp had grown significantly, the board had decided to bring in some help. He was just keeping me up to date on progress for the upcoming session, and I was almost disappointed that there was so little for me to do. But I had another message that would prove a better distraction.

Solamentes: golf.

That was very Mario. One word. It was a question, a statement. A plan, maybe? He'd included me, Van Porter, Cade Simpson, and Tyler Cornwall on the text, and by the time I was sitting down with a couple eggs and some turkey bacon, Simpson had responded.

Simpson: Yes.

Van: When and where?

Corny: Come to the club.

Cornwall's parents were loaded, and he didn't mind taking advantage and making sure his teammates all got the chance too. I was pretty sure his dad actually owned the country club, though maybe his name was just on everything because he was some kind of major sponsor.

I had no clue.

All that mattered to me was that the invite had come at the perfect time. I needed distraction. And while a day spent with teammates definitely wouldn't be a day without a lot of hockey talk, it would be a break from the skates.

Me: I'm in.

Simpson: Sams, pick me up on your way. I'm at my sister's place.

We'd figured out that Cade's sister lived just around the corner from the house I'd bought recently. She was married and had three or four kids, and Cade seemed to spend a lot of his off time there being their favorite uncle.

Me: Sure. Time?

Solamentes: noon.

I hoped there was a lot of shade on Corny's course. It was already tipping over ninety degrees, and it was barely ten in the morning.

Unable to stop myself, I did a quick workout in the garage—a little time on the tread and some biceps and back —and then I hit the shower and headed out to pick up Simpson at his sister's place.

"Sams!" he boomed as he slid into the passenger seat of my truck wearing a bright pink shirt I'd never have imagined him wearing.

"Hey, Cade. Nice shirt, man."

"Real men wear pink, John." We did a quick fist bump and I pulled out from the curb as three red-headed kids waved from the front window of the house.

"How's your family?"

"Nuts, man. The best thing about your sister having kids is you can go get 'em all riled up and then run away." He cackled, the sound coming from somewhere beneath the impressive red beard he sported. Simpson was huge and intimidating on the ice, but I'd gotten to know him well enough to know that he was a teddy bear in real life. Not that I was planning to give him a squeeze or anything, but the guy had a heart of gold.

We picked up Cade's clubs at his condo and then drove out to the country club on the far side of Wilcox and pulled into the lot next to the over-the-top silver corvette Solamentes drove. He was waiting, leaning against the hood, which he rubbed with the hem of his shirt when he stood.

"How's your precious baby?" Simpson asked him, laughing.

"Good as long as you don't door ding her," he answered. "How's it going, Sams?"

"Good," I told him, locking the truck after pulling the clubs out of the back. "Glad you texted. I needed to take a day off."

"You been working hard?" he asked, eyeing me up and down.

"I mean, no. Well, yeah, but like... off-season hard." I sensed I was about to get the same lecture Mizzoni had offered, so I tried to make it seem like I was vacationing, enjoying the time.

"Right." Mario Solamentes was a man of few words, but you could read most of his thoughts in his expressions. The one he wore now told me he knew I was full of shit.

We headed into the club to find Corny and Van Porter finishing up at the desk. Corny tossed a set of cart keys to Simpson. "Let's head."

We divided into two groups and rode out onto the course in our fancy golf carts, which moved almost fast enough to create a tiny breeze to offset the stifling humidity. Virginia summers were hot, though they were nothing compared to where I grew up in the deep South. Still, it was a relief when the bar cart showed up around the third hole.

We had a couple big thermoses of water, and now we supplemented those with cocktails, each of us doing our best to outhit the others. I wasn't a natural golfer, but I enjoyed the game. There was no real point trying to compete with guys like Corny and Solamentes, anyway. It was clear they'd both grown up with clubs in their hands. Simpson did okay, mostly through sheer force, but his putting game was shit.

"You hit the ball like it's a puck, man," Corny pointed out as Simpson tried for his fourth putt around the sixth hole.

"Can't help it. Besides, you want me to perfect my putting or keep my shot strong on the ice?"

"Ice!" we all agreed.

The day slipped by in a haze of greenery, gin and tonics, and camaraderie, and by the time we finished up and sat down to grab burgers in the bar, my mind had let go of some of the angst I'd carried out of last season.

The guys were talking about putting together a weekend at a lake house owned by another teammate, and we were all laughing and relaxed. I almost didn't feel my phone vibrate in my pocket, but managed to answer on the last ring.

The screen read "Wilcox County Sheriff." What was this?

"Hello?"

"John Samuels?"

"Uh, yeah. Who's this?"

"Hey there. Sorry to bother you, Wilcox County sheriff's department here. Listen, we brought in a prowler one of your neighbors reported, caught nosing around the side of your house, trying windows and whatnot."

"Seriously?" I lived in a pretty small house. I hadn't thought it would be a burglary target. "Anything stolen?"

"No, uh, she didn't make it inside."

"She?"

"We're thinking this could be a stalking situation. You being a pro athlete and everything."

A stalker? I definitely didn't think I was famous enough for that. "Uh, okay. So what do you need from me?"

"Well again, sorry to bother you with this, but this woman... she's just really feisty."

"Okay..."

"She swears she knows you and is reaching for the phone as we speak." His voice lowered to a whisper, like he was ducking away to keep the phone out of her grasp and hissing into it. "She's kind of bossy."

Who the heck did I know in Wilcox that would be prowling around my house? And who was also bossy?

"She wants to speak with you. She says it will clear everything up. I told her this is highly unusual, but—"

"Put her on," I suggested, giving a shrug to the guys at the table who were all listening now.

Shuffling sounded on the other end, and then came a sweet Southern voice I hadn't heard in years. "Sammy? Is that you?"

"Joey?"

"Yes! It's me. I'm so sorry about all this! Everything's been totally blown out of proportion."

My best friend from high school had been caught stalking me? "Um, Joey, what's going on? Were you prowling outside my house? How did you know where I live?"

"It's a long story, really. But I came up here to Wilcox hoping to see you."

"Through the window I bet," the cop's voice said in the distance.

"Uh, okay, well, I'm gonna be heading home here soon. Do you want to come back over? I can let you inside this time?"

"That's the thing. These guys hauled me to the police station and they won't let me go until you tell them you don't want to press any charges or anything. I think they're getting ready to make me change into an orange jumpsuit here."

"Should I come get you?"

"Oh, would you? They made me ride in the cruiser, so my car is at your house. The sheriff here is really dedicated to his job, I guess."

The Wilcox sheriff was notoriously underworked and overzealous, rarely following the same protocols those in bigger cities seemed to adhere to.

Simpson was practically leaning over my plate now, trying to figure out what was going on, and I was a little worried about his beard getting into my food.

"Sams, you're being rude," Solamentes said, reaching over and helping himself to some of my fries. I moved the plate a little closer to my body.

"Sorry," I whispered to the guys. "Joey, hang tight. I'll be right there, okay?"

"Thanks, Sammy. I'm really so, so sorry about this."

"Yeah, it's no problem."

There was more shuffling on the phone, then the cop's voice came back on. "We'll detain the suspect until you arrive, Mr. Samuels. Sorry for the trouble."

"Sure. Yeah, I'll be there soon."

Joey Baxter was in Wilcox? My head spun as I hung up and explained quickly. "My best friend from high school got picked up by the cops trying to break into my house or something. I need to head to the police station."

"Dude sounds a little unhinged," Simpson said. "You want me to come with you in case this Joey guy's gone off his rocker since you were in school?"

"Ah, no. Actually, Joey's a girl. Josephine."

Eyebrows went up around the table.

"Can you get a ride with one of these guys, Cade?"

"Sure, man." He stuffed some of my fries in his mouth. I thought about asking for a to go box for the few fries that remained and decided against it. I pushed the plate into the center of the table.

"Be careful," Corny said.

I'd never needed to be careful around Joey. Of everyone I'd ever known, she was the one person I was most myself with. Or I had been, until we'd gone our separate ways for college and lost touch. "Yeah, I will be." I was already out of my seat, heading for the car.

Why was Joey here? And why did some part of me rush to grab a shovel and start digging up long-buried fantasies that involved my old pal Josephine Baxter finally realizing that we could be so much more than friends?

CHAPTER 4
JOEY

CRIME EVERYWHERE YOU LOOK

So far my escape to freedom had been exhilarating, exhausting, and embarrassing, all rolled up into one less-than twenty-four hour period. It did seem like we were hanging on embarrassing for longer than necessary, though.

"You're a long way from home, miss." The lanky, bald-headed cop who'd picked me up still had my phone, and was examining my credit cards and driver's license for the four-millionth time. "Alabama, huh?" He grinned at me, as if this was some private joke I was in on. I wasn't sure why Alabama was funny, but he was irritatingly amused.

"People do leave the state now and then," I said, my efforts to remain polite beginning to fail me in the face of my need to sleep. And eat. And pee.

He closed my phone case and dropped it to the desk he occupied just outside the bars of the holding cell. At least I was alone inside the cell. I didn't get the sense that Wilcox was a hotspot for crime, based on the excitement my prowling offenses seemed to have caused here. Clearly there was no one nearby doing anything more serious to warrant police attention.

"Why did you leave the state?" the guy asked.

I had been working exceptionally hard not to think about why I left Alabama. Or about the phone the guy had picked up yet again to peer at. I'd turned it off as soon as I'd spoken to Evan and typed out a text to my mother, and now I peered at it like a bomb sitting in the palm of the guy's hand. I'd also been trying hard not to think about what might be going on back in Peach Tree Grove right now or about whether or not there had been bed bugs in the mattress of the room I'd rented overnight at the Boomsmack Motel. I was itchy. And the bathroom in that place had not instilled enough confidence in me to risk taking a shower there. I probably smelled.

"You not talking now?" the cop asked, giving me a narrow-eyed look through the bars.

"Sorry, no. I'm just tired. Is this like, an official police interview? Do I have to answer? Should I get a lawyer, maybe?"

The man's mouth dropped open and he leaned back as if I'd slapped him. "Just making conversation, ma'am."

"Samuels is here," a voice came through the door to the front that popped open and then slammed shut again.

Relief washed through me, but a second later, a little spike of nervous fear followed. I hadn't seen Sammy since high school. I came home for holidays and summers, but once he left for college, he never came back. We'd kept in touch via text for a while, but he was so absorbed in hockey and studying... and I'd begun dating Evan.

What would he be like now?

I knew only that he was playing professionally now, and that he played for a team here, in Wilcox. I'd seen him once on television, and his photo had come up when I'd dug around for an address, but I wasn't sure how recent it might be. Still, the thought of John Samuels brought me a sense of comfort, just as it always had. Sammy was one of the good guys.

"Come on back," a voice said from the door, which was opening again. Another cop came through, this one with a shaggy mullet and an extremely dark tan, and behind him —John Samuels.

I felt my face break into a smile the second his eyes found mine, but my happiness faded at the confused look on his face.

"Joey?" he stepped up closer to the bars.

"Hi Sammy." Suddenly, humiliation bolted through me, making me shrink into myself. I dropped his gaze. The man on the other side of the holding cell bars looked like my high school friend, but he was also completely different. The man who stood there was at least four inches taller, had broad shoulders and bulging biceps I didn't remember at all, and a shock of dark hair that was short around the sides and perfectly mussed on top. He was painfully handsome, and it only served to make me more self-conscious.

I was a bedraggled mess, and I was currently behind bars.

"This is crazy," he said, his voice full of confusion and a

little bit of wonder. "Hey, can we let her out of the cell? She's not a criminal, clearly."

"So you can identify this woman?" the tall cop asked, crossing his arms over his chest and puffing it out as he approached John.

John's size and stature made both men look little, like early attempts at men that had been abandoned once the sculptor had created John.

"Yes, I know her. This is all a mistake. She's not a criminal. Let her out, please."

"Okay, but if there's another incident, I won't say I didn't see it coming." The bald cop reluctantly opened the cell door as my eyes met John's again to find a hint of amusement there.

A giggle escaped me, and I slapped a hand over my mouth.

"She's hysterical now," the tanned cop noted, frowning at me through his very dense mustache.

"No, I'm fine, sorry." I stepped out the open door of the cell, smoothing the sundress I'd been wearing since my fitting the day before. "Just... I don't even know what I am." I sighed, suddenly close to tears, but John put an arm over my shoulders then and pulled me to his side. I nearly burst into tears at the simple reassurance he offered without even thinking about it.

It felt like it had been years since someone had cared enough about how I felt to offer a gesture of reassurance like that.

"Do you have all your stuff?" John's voice was soft, calm, and understanding.

"My phone..." I pointed to the bald cop holding my phone.

John held a hand out to the man, and he deposited the sparkly pink case into it, making the phone look slightly ridiculous and John's hand look enormous.

"Is she free to go, gentlemen? Do I need to sign anything?"

"No sir," said the bald cop. "Just see that your girlfriend there doesn't find herself prowling around any other sports stars' houses, will ya?" He shook his head and looked to the other cop as we headed for the door. "Heard about some kind of hot tub squatting incident last winter too. What's Wilcox coming to?"

"Crime everywhere you look," the first cop said.

John kept his arm around me as we left the back room and exited through the lobby. When we emerged from the station into the swampy summer heat of late afternoon, he stopped us on the sidewalk and turned to face me, his hands remaining on my shoulders for a brief moment.

"Joey Baxter." A wide smile overtook his handsome face, making the dark eyes sparkle. He pulled a pair of sunglasses from his collar and put them on, making him even more handsome. "I'm guessing there's a good story here."

"I don't know about that," I told him. Seeing John was comforting, and I let the warm reassurance his presence had always given me settle my nerves.

"Well it's good to see you, anyway," he laughed. He helped me up into the passenger side of a huge black truck, and soon we were seated side by side, the air conditioning blasting as we drove through downtown Wilcox.

"Thanks for coming to get me," I said, wishing my voice was a little stronger, more confident, but I was second-guessing my mad dash to Virginia. John had a life here. What had I been thinking, just showing up? Oh god. What if John was married?

I glanced at his hand on the steering wheel—no ring. But that didn't mean no girlfriend. Or fiancée. I cringed thinking about how I'd just assumed he would be here, ready to take me in. A lot of time had passed.

"I'll bust you out of jail anytime, Joey." John's easy manner relaxed me a little. He was the same in that way— In high school he'd had a way of making me see that things were okay, that the details I stressed about weren't impor- tant, that life was good. Maybe that was why he was the person I'd run to now. "Let's head to my place and you can tell me what's been going on for the last... what, five years?"

"Are you sure you have time? I kind of just showed up here. Will your, uh...girlfriend mind?"

John laughed. "No girlfriend. My cat Hank might be a little put out. He's used to being my one and only."

Relief was like a cool breeze. That was good. I was already an intrusion. I didn't want to be a third wheel.

"Best surprise I've had in a while, minus maybe the police station part," he said, turning to shoot that smile at me again.

A little more tension left my body. "Really?"

"I'm happy to see you, Joey. And it's the off-season, so I have some time to spare."

He seemed sincere, so I decided to accept his words at face value and let go of a tiny bit of the uncertainty I'd begun to feel over my snap decision to come here. I'd missed my friend, and if he was willing to visit for a bit, that would give me time to figure out what I was going to do next.

John pointed at my phone on the center console. "If it's dead, you can charge it here." He reached for the charge cord connected to the dash.

"Oh, no, that's okay. I think I'd rather leave it off a bit longer."

His face changed, his mouth quirking to one side and his eyebrows lowering behind his shades, but if John thought it was odd I didn't want my phone working, he didn't say anything else about it.

"This is me," he said, pulling up a narrow driveway to a one-car garage attached to a small ranch-style house. "But I guess you knew that," he laughed.

"Yeah, sorry." I glanced at the enormous silver SUV parked in front of his house. "That's me. The cops said they were going to impound it, but I guess they didn't get that far."

John let out a low whistle. "Nice ride."

A prick of discomfort sealed my lips shut. That had always been the one thing between us that didn't lay quite flat. Daddy's money had been a silent reminder of just how different we were. And while I'd never been a girl to flaunt the wealth I'd grown up with, it had been impossible in the amount of time John and I spent together not to feel the disparity. Things I didn't think twice about were out of reach for him sometimes.

But here we were, in his blingy black truck, pulling into the garage of his house. He was a professional hockey player now. And most likely, I was about to be disinherited. Maybe the tables had turned.

None of that had ever mattered to me anyway.

John parked the car and came around to help me out.

"Thanks," I said, unable to meet his eyes again. The day was crashing in on me, the reality of what I'd done beginning to overtake the adrenaline-fueled drive and fear-soaked night I'd spent.

"Let's go inside and you can tell me what's going on, okay?"

I nodded and followed him inside his house, increasingly nervous as I realized how insane all of this was.

"Can I get you anything? Something to drink? You hungry?"

John had led the way to a small but modern kitchen and pulled a water pitcher from the refrigerator. He filled two glasses and handed me one before I'd managed an answer.

"Thanks. Um, actually, maybe a shower." I felt sticky and damp, and like the accumulated fear and adrenaline might be clinging to me now.

John smiled, putting his water back on the kitchen counter. "Yeah, of course. I've got a guest room here with an en suite bathroom. Should be towels and everything you need in there." He led the way to the other side of the house, down a little hall to a bright and welcoming room decorated in yellow and white.

"Thank you," I said, stepping in and wishing the Boomsmack motel had been half as nice. John had great taste. I turned back to him. "I'll get cleaned up and then I promise, I'll explain."

"There's no rush, Joey. I'm curious, but I'm not going anywhere. Take your time."

As John turned and left, shutting the door behind him, all the jittering nervous things inside me calmed down just a little. In a very strange way, I felt like I was home.

I forced myself to take a deep calming breath, letting it out slowly, and then stepped into the bathroom and closed the door behind me.

CHAPTER 5

JOHN

THE DANGER OF THE SPARKLY PHONE

I walked slowly back out to the kitchen and picked up my water, downing it in one long swallow as my mind worked through the last hour.

Hank appeared from the living room and plopped down in front of me, letting out a mewl and putting one paw on my shoe. His way of asking for attention. I leaned down and scooped him up, nestling him against my chest and fondling his soft ears while I thought.

Josephine Baxter was suddenly at my house. In my shower.

I wasn't at all disappointed about it—my best friend was still the prettiest girl I'd ever seen, and the second I'd locked eyes with her I'd felt that same protective instinct spring to life inside me. I just didn't know why she was here, or for how long. But I'd find out pretty soon, I guessed.

While she showered, I pulled a few things from the refrigerator, putting together a plate of cheese and crackers, salami, some olives and some pickles. I had no idea when she'd eaten last—despite her eternal beauty, Joey had looked a little worse for wear and could probably use some calories. As I was staring into the freezer trying to figure out if I had any actual food that could be combined into a halfway appropriate dinner, I heard the guest room door click open again. I shut the freezer and turned, and felt my eyes grow wide as every cell in my body suddenly sprang to attention.

Joey stood in my living room in only a towel. Her tanned arms clutched the top to her chest, and miles of long, gorgeous leg showed beneath the too-short hem. My heart rate ticked up and I swallowed hard.

I made a mental note, somewhere in the far, deep reaches of my brain that were still operating in the face of all that skin, to buy bigger bath towels for the guest room. What was scarcely covering Joey's body might have been supposed to be an oversized hand towel, now that I got a good look at it.

"I...uh, I don't have any other clothes," Joey said, her voice a little shaky.

I ripped my eyes from the spot where the towel threatened to slip down the swell of her breasts and tried to look nonchalant. "Oh!" I walked toward her, but she was blocking my path to the back of the house.

"I can get you some..." I moved to the right, but Joey moved at the same time. We both reversed directions, still blocking each other. It was like the uncomfortable dance you did with strangers on the sidewalk, when neither of you could seem to choose the right way to go. "I'll just, uh..." I reached out both hands, grasping Joey's warm shoulders, and urged her gently to one side. "I'll just get you some things," I said, slipping past her to get to my own room at the end of the hall.

The Wombats T-shirt would certainly be too big, and so would the shorts, but hopefully they'd work for now. I handed them to her, and she clutched them against the towel that was threatening to slip. I did my best to keep my eyes high. "These are the best I've got for now," I told her.

"This is perfect. Thank you, Sammy."

As she disappeared back into the guest room, her voice replayed in my head. It was different, I thought. Joey had been on top of the world in high school, master of her universe. But this version of my best friend sounded timid, uncertain. Not Joey-like at all. What had happened in these last five years to change her?

When she emerged again from the guest room, her hair in a knot atop her head and her body swallowed by my clothes, I had to push down the misplaced pride I felt seeing her in my stuff. She was not here for me. Something was clearly going on with Joey, and for whatever reason, this was the only place she'd had to go. I shoved away the attraction and desire I felt, just as I'd had to do every day back in school.

"Better?" I asked, thinking silently that the Wombats shirt looked much better on her than it ever had on me.

She smiled and moved back to pick up the water she'd abandoned. "Much better." She drank the water, and I waved her to the couch.

"Need anything else? I made some snacks."

"Oh my god, that looks amazing. I'm starving." She sat

down and immediately folded a piece of salami and cheese atop a cracker and took a bite. I was about to sit when she spoke again, cracker crumbs flying from her lips as she looked up at me. "Sammy?"

Her eyes were shining and huge, and she looked suddenly innocent and so young, having washed her makeup off in the shower. "Yeah?"

"Do you have any whiskey?"

I didn't keep a lot of booze in the house, but Rock Stevens was a big fan of this whiskey he'd found back in Maryland, and he handed it out whenever he visited anyone on the team. "I do, actually." I brought the bottle of Half Cat Whiskey to the coffee table and set it down with a glass. "Need ice?"

"That's okay. Thanks."

Joey poured herself a healthy four or five fingers as I sat.

I watched her take a sip and then a gulp, and finally set the glass down and fix me in her blue-eyed gaze. "I'm sure you're wondering what the heck I'm doing here."

"I'd be lying if I said I wasn't curious."

I sank into the seat catty-corner to hers and watched as she seemed to pull herself together and assemble her thoughts. "I guess the easiest explanation is to tell you I've run away."

I leaned forward. "From..."

"From home." She sipped at her whiskey.

"Uh, okay." It wasn't quite the explanation I'd been looking for, given that she was at least twenty-two, but I decided to be patient. Surely there was more coming.

"I'm certain Mama's in a panic and Daddy's probably

going to disinherit me now." The words were calm, but her voice cracked as she spoke and her eyes filled.

"So... you're still living at home?"

She nodded, a strand of long blond hair escaping the bun and dropping to trail along her cheek. "Pathetic, I know." Her eyes found mine and a single tear slipped down her cheek. "Oh Sammy. I want to tell you that I went to college and did all the things we talked about—majored in science, found a great career, and threw off the bonds of my debutante upbringing." She used air quotes for this last part and generally looked so miserable I wanted to reach out to console her. But it was clear she wasn't finished.

Joey took another healthy swig of whiskey and kept talking.

"But that's not what happened at all. I don't know if it's genetic or just the way my parents brainwashed me growing up with all the talk about a lady's proper place in the world—"

"You never bought into any of that," I pointed out. I remembered Joey vividly in high school swearing she'd never become her mother, never limit her world to entertaining and being a wife and mother. She wanted more. She'd always wanted something else.

"But I did," she said, dropping my gaze. "I must have," she said sadly. "Because in college, Evan Stratton and I started dating. And he proposed when I was a junior. And I said yes."

I glanced at her left hand, there was no ring there. Relief washed through me, though I shouldn't have cared if she was engaged, or married even.

"Evan Stratton, huh?" He'd been the quarterback on our high school team when we were freshmen. He'd graduated a couple years ahead of us. I'd never known the guy, but his family was huge in Peach Tree Grove. His dad had some important law firm, and his uncle was the mayor.

"Yes. And then it was like the wheels were set in motion. And everything just proceeded along a set path, like I had no say in anything at all."

"Did you stay in school?" I asked. I couldn't imagine Joey dropping out to get married.

"Yes. I graduated last June. And every day since then has been about plotting the next steps."

I imagined job interviews and career plans—Joey had always wanted to study genetics and go into healthcare. But she was still talking, and she wasn't describing mapping genomes or studying biostatistics.

"Flowers, invitations, venues...it never ended. From the day I graduated, Mama took control, and the wedding machine was rolling ahead, steamrolling everything in its path."

I shook my head, still not quite tracking. "So you're married?"

It was her turn to shake her head. She sighed and picked up the glass once more, downing the rest of the whiskey within it. "I'm not," she said, setting the glass down hard. "But I would be. If I hadn't run."

"You ran away from your wedding?"

"I did."

"Did you leave poor Evan at the altar?" I asked, picturing the star athlete gazing around at the entire town of Peach Tree Grove, humiliated. The thought didn't upset me much, and I immediately felt bad for wishing anything like that for him.

"No. I wouldn't do that. At least, I don't think I would. I dropped my mother off after my final dress fitting and just kept driving. I was in Georgia by the time the rehearsal dinner should have been going. And when I should have been at the church? I was facedown at the Boomsmack Motel."

"What? The Motel?" Had someone forced her there? Hurt her?

"Your reaction is warranted. That place is seedy as heck. But I went there by choice. It was the first place I saw, and I was exhausted. It was the middle of the night, and I didn't want to come straight here and wake you up. I wasn't even sure I had your address right."

"So that's why you were prowling around? To figure out if this was the right house?"

She chuckled. "Yeah. I woke up late—I hadn't meant to oversleep, but I guess I needed it. And then I came here."

"How'd you get my address?"

She lifted a shoulder, reaching for another piece of cheese. "You can find almost anything online now, you know."

That was concerning. "Oh."

For a beat, neither of us said anything, but once I'd absorbed the how and why of her showing up here suddenly, my mind began to inch toward the potential repercussions of her flight from Alabama.

"So your family is pretty upset? And Evan?"

She shrugged. "Haven't talked to any of them since I left. I called Evan and sent Mama a text. My phone's been off since then, except for mapping here."

I let out a low whistle. "That's some pretty impressive self-control."

"Extreme fear, more like."

I nodded, glancing at the sparkly pink phone face down on the table and cringing slightly at the kinds of messages that were probably waiting there for Joey.

"So, what's the plan now?"

She fell back against the couch, her face crumpling for the briefest of seconds before she said simply, "I have no idea." Then she dropped her big eyes shut and blew out a little breath. "I'm really sorry, John. Maybe I shouldn't have come here. I didn't know where to go."

"Hey," I said, waiting until those bright blue eyes met mine again. "First of all, I'm glad you came. It's great to see you again. Second, you're welcome to stay as long as you want. As long as it takes to figure things out."

I'd expected a thank you, maybe even hoped for a hug. But Joey just melted into the couch as a tiny sob escaped her and she dropped her head onto her arms, curling herself into a ball atop the cushions. "Oh Sammy, what am I going to do?" Her voice was a muffled moan, and it twisted my stomach in sympathetic misery.

Joey's shoulders shook and her back heaved as she cried, and I sat frozen there, panic creeping in around the edges of my consciousness. Crying women were one of the things I most feared. I didn't grow up with women—except this one, really, and I'd never known her to cry when we were younger.

"Hey," I said softly, standing to go to her. I dropped a hand on her back and rubbed gently in circles, feeling slightly ridiculous. Is this what you did for crying women? "Hey, it's gonna be okay," I tried again.

Joey shifted, and the next thing I knew, her head was in my lap, her tears soaking the khakis I'd worn to golf, as I stroked her back up and down while she continued to sob. My day had definitely taken an odd turn. One thing I could not have predicted was the unrequited high school crush I'd never really gotten over showing up and then molding herself into my lap as she cried.

I held her, forcing my body to remain relaxed, calm—she needed reassurance not attraction. But shit, Joey was—*still was*—the most attractive woman I'd ever known. And seeing her dressed in my oversized shirt and shorts did nothing to reduce the pull I felt to her. What Joey wore didn't matter because the things I'd loved about her had always been deeper than her looks.

My hand rubbed up and down her back as I thought about my long-time friend. I'd missed her, I realized. But I also didn't want to get too invested in the idea of Joey being back in my life... I had no idea what her plans might be.

Eventually, the tears subsided, and Joey sat up, looking miserably at the dark spot on my pants.

"Sorry," she sniffed. Both her hands went to her face then, rubbing up and over her hair. "I'm such a mess."

"It's okay," I said. "Seriously."

The sun had drifted lower as we sat there, and my

stomach was beginning to growl. I wasn't sure what the right thing would be in this situation, but I knew I needed to eat something more than cheese and crackers. And maybe Joey needed some distraction.

"Hey," I tried. "Want to see some of the town? I could take you out to dinner."

Joey stared at me and then her eyes drifted down to the Wombats shirt she wore and the baggy shorts. "I doubt I'm dressed for dinner."

Clothes. Right. That would be an issue.

"There's a Target down the road," I told her. "We could pop by on the way and grab some things for you."

"I haven't been in a Target since college," she said, her eyes widening. "Mama wouldn't hear of going there, but I love Target."

"Great," I said. "Let me take a quick shower and we'll go."

For the first time since we'd arrived at my house, Joey smiled. And for a second, I glimpsed the strong-willed, ferocious girl I used to know. I didn't know how long she'd be here, or what was going to happen, but in that second, I told myself that I'd do whatever I could to bring that girl back for good.

CHAPTER 6
JOEY

THE WONDERS OF TARGET

Target was one of my favorite places in the world —a wonder of disparate items of every kind, all set together in one enormous store. Peach Tree Grove didn't have any of what I think were referred to as "big box" stores, and spending the last year back there with my parents was a lot like going back in time. We could always go to Montgomery for all the big stores, but Mama hated places like this.

"A store should do one thing and do it well. I don't want to buy my unmentionables from a place selling tuna fish two aisles over." Mama was easily offended by things like that.

On the other hand, I adored the possibility of picking up an affordable temporary wardrobe, skin care, a toothbrush, makeup, and several bottles of Prosecco all in one place.

John waited patiently as I shopped, strolling along the wide aisles at my side. He practically glowed with good-ness, and I realized it was why I'd run here. To him. John stood apart in my mind from everyone else I'd ever known.

His family had been a little tough—not a lot of love there, I didn't think—but it didn't keep him from being one of the most honest, forthright, easygoing people I'd ever known. It was just nice to be around him.

Though being around this version of John Samuels was different. My high school pal was gone—or at least his body was. This John was unquestionably a man. One with impressive muscles and a chiseled jaw that carried just a trace of dark scruff. And just out of the shower? This version of John smelled like heaven, if heaven had a tiny bit of sin mixed in. He was sexy.

But that wasn't why I'd come to him.

We were friends. And right now? I really needed a friend.

It wasn't that I didn't have girlfriends. The problem was that they were all involved in the wedding, and for the moment I'd needed to just set that entire situation aside. I would have to deal with it. Just not right now.

I tried on clothes for the better part of an hour.

"It's amazing what a variety they have here," I told John, modeling a pair of dark jeans in front of the mirror. "I'm finding so much!"

"Good," he called back through the door. "I'm glad you're happy."

In that brief second, I was. But the reality of what I'd just done to my life was lingering in the distance, a dark, swirling storm threatening to blow in soon.

I pulled the tags from the jeans and a cropped, V-neck T-shirt, and slipped my feet into a pair of cute sneakers. It was miles better than the baggy shorts and T-shirt with strappy sandals look I'd been sporting from John's house.

"I think I've got what I need," I told John, emerging from the dressing room feeling better. Brighter.

"Good," he said. "Let's find something to eat. I'm starving."

As I watched the checkout girl scan all my items. My eyes wandered the assortment of vendors just along the front of the store. "We could get a pretzel here," I told John, pointing to the concession.

"I was thinking something more like a steak. I don't think they sell those at Target."

As the girl bagged the last of my items, I slipped my credit card from my phone case and paid. Until the little machine flashed "approved," I held my breath. There was a good chance Daddy would switch off my card, but it didn't seem like he'd done it yet. I checked the cash back option and withdrew some money just in case. I hoped the cards would work for a bit longer, that my parents were waiting to talk to me, to convince me to come back.

But I also knew I couldn't go back. I couldn't step into the life they had planned for me, the one I'd been so easily complicit in planning for myself.

Being here, away from the life I'd slipped back into so easily after school, I thought I felt a flicker of that thing I'd had once before. Drive, or motivation. Desire. I felt my heart and soul waking up and realizing there were things only I could secure for myself.

"Dinner," John said, hoisting my bags into the back seat of the cab of his truck.

"Sounds good," I said. "My treat."

"Don't be silly."

We settled into the cab, and after I strapped my seatbelt, I turned to look at him, catching that dark, chocolate gaze. Soulful. Sexy. Something stirred low in my gut that felt like attraction, but I shoved it down. This was neither the time nor place for that kind of thought.

"Listen. I owe you," I told him. "And I'm guessing it won't be long before these cards I've got are going to become useless, so let me buy you dinner. Please."

A slow smile crept across the full lips, and he shook his head lightly. "If you insist, but it doesn't feel very gentlemanly."

John *was* a gentleman, I thought. He always had been. And even though his accent had faded and he'd moved north, I knew he had the same values I'd been brought up with. Letting me buy him dinner was a lot.

"You've already demonstrated that you are a gentleman in a million ways, Sammy. You got me out of jail, and you're letting me stay at your house. You let me cry and took me shopping. And honestly? I don't need a gentleman right now. I just need my friend."

He grinned as he navigated through the darkening streets of Wilcox. "You got it," he said.

Dinner was simple but delicious. We settled into a table at the back of a cozy bistro and John got his steak while I had a delicious French onion soup and a salad. We both drank water, but when John started asking questions about things back home, I began wishing for something stronger.

"Where was the wedding supposed to be, Joey?"

"The ceremony was at St. John's, and the reception was going to be at the Robert E. Lee."

"As one does," John said.

I burst out laughing. "As one's mama does."

"Was there going to be any kind of civil war re-enactment?"

I dropped my fork to stare at him, pretending to be offended. "No."

"Your dad was pretty into that, wasn't he?"

"Yes, but he agreed to leave it out of the wedding." Daddy had asked if he should call some of his friends to bring their uniforms, but Mama had nipped that idea in the bud. "Mama really did all the planning. I just had to show up," I told him, thinking of the whole thing as if it was someone else's wedding now. In a way, it had been.

"Did you get to plan any part of it?" John was watching me, those dark perceptive eyes shining in the light of the little candle glowing between us on the table.

I lifted a shoulder, my brain working back through all the decisions that had been made in the last year. "Mama always consulted me, of course," I said, trying to remember if I'd actually chosen anything. "But I guess she just gave me choices she'd already selected, so there was never a wrong answer."

"Sounds like it was going to be her wedding."

I nodded, some of the anxiety I'd felt at home threat-ening to creep back in as we talked about the details of the event.

"And what about Evan?"

"He didn't plan anything."

"That's not what I'm asking." John's expression was hard to read. Did he feel sorry for Evan? Did he think I'd done something cruel, running away? His brow was smooth, the eyes open and questioning, but not judging.

"What are you asking?"

"Do you love him?"

I couldn't hold John's gaze. How could I admit I was a day away from marrying a man I didn't know if I loved?

"Maybe?" I tried, realizing as the word escaped that it was weak and inadequate. "I mean, I think I did."

John was watching me when I glanced at him again, like he was trying to figure something out.

"I know it's the wrong answer," I said, my voice an embarrassed breath.

"I guess I don't have any expertise in love," John said, leaning back and pushing his plate away. "I've never been in love. But I like to think I'd know if I was."

"Me too." I dropped my eyes to my silverware, tumbling the knife over a couple times before finding the courage to ask the next question. "What do you think it's like? How do you think you would know?"

"I like to think it'd be so obvious—to both of us—that it would be impossible to deny it. That love would be like drinking water for the first time, never realizing how much you'd actually needed it. Or like pulling off a blindfold and understanding that you'd spent the first part of your life not really seeing anything."

"Sammy, you've become a poet." I laughed, but his words were like an arrow, finding a soft target inside me and lodging there. I'd once thought love should be like that too. But if it was, I'd never felt it.

A little blush crept up his cheeks, making him even more handsome as he chuckled and fussed with the spoon next to his plate, obviously embarrassed.

"I hope you're right," I told him. "And that maybe it isn't too late for me. But no. I don't love Evan like that."

John looked at me then, and there was something so comforting and familiar in his eyes, that any doubt I'd had about whether coming here was the right move was instantly gone. I'd needed my best friend, and even though there were years and miles between us, seeing him again was right. And I was home.

"Think you should listen to those messages?" John asked as we pulled back into his driveway.

"I'm not sure you have enough whiskey for that," I said as dread pooled inside me, snaking cold fingers around my heart and making me shiver despite the heat. I could imagine my mother's furious voice, Evan's confusion and hurt, the humiliation I'd caused them all. Could I really bear hearing it?

I squared my shoulders and took a deep breath. I was the one who'd run. I was the one who'd caused the hurt and embarrassment. I would have to take what came with that.

Inside, John brought new glasses to the coffee table where the bottle of whiskey still stood. He filled them both and we drank, my phone sparkling on the table between us like a glittery bright bomb that would soon explode.

I lifted my glass and drank, and then I hit the power button on my phone.

"I have seventeen voice messages and over one hundred unread texts," I said, watching the screen update as the evidence of my quick decision making loaded.

Sammy's eyes stayed steady on mine, offering warmth and confidence where I felt my own slipping.

"We'll do it like you eat an elephant," he said. His voice was like warm chocolate, which didn't change the fact that his words were ridiculous.

"I don't know where you've been these last five years, Sammy, but we don't eat many elephants in the South so I'm not sure I know how that would be done." I stared back down at the phone screen, fear twerking with guilt center-stage in my gut.

"If you were to eat an elephant, how would you do it?"

"Are you just trying to distract me with this? It is working, but it's a little bizarre." I put the phone in my lap and met his eyes, which sparkled with amusement now.

"It is actually an idiom, Joey. I didn't just make it up. And you start a little bit at a time." He held out his hand and I happily gave him the phone. "If you want, I'll help. Where do you want to start? Messages or texts?"

"Texts, I think. Less terrifying." I took another big drink of my whiskey and then picked up a pillow from the couch, holding it in my lap as if it might absorb some of the piercing words I knew were about to come my way.

"Want me to read them aloud for you?"

I had no secrets from Sammy. He already knew the worst of me. I was a grown woman who'd run away from her own wedding because she was too weak and powerless to just tell everyone it wasn't what she wanted. How much less could he think of me now after he'd already had this truth confirmed?

"Yes please." I gripped the pillow tightly and waited.

"Okay. You've got messages here from Tess, Mama, Daddy, Evan, Sarah, Aunt Maud, and Granny T."

Granny. Oh god, I should have called Granny. It was a lot for her to get all dressed up and go anywhere at eighty-eight, and she might've appreciated knowing she didn't have to get dolled up for the rehearsal dinner. Besides that, she was probably the one person in that list who wasn't going to tell me I was a horrible person.

"Start with Granny T, please."

John smiled up at me. "How is Granny T? You two still like peas and carrots?" I thought I'd heard a faint southern drawl when he asked me this, and it loosened a tiny bit of the tension inside me. The rough southern boy with good manners I'd known was still in there somewhere.

"Always," I told him. "Granny T just gets me. She always has. I should've told her what I was doing." I moaned the last part, guilt beginning to win the dance off with fear inside me.

"Okay. Her text says, 'Dear Josephine,'" Sammy paused, grinning. "Very formal for a text."

"Just be impressed that Granny texts at all. She's more adept with that phone of hers than I am." My heart squeezed a little thinking about my Granny. I wished I could give her a hug right then. I should have called her.

"I'm not surprised," Sammy said. He'd met Granny T many times over the years. "'Dear Josephine, I wish we'd had a chance to chat before you made your mad dash out of

Peach Tree Grove. I would've told you to run faster. Don't worry about things here. Granny T is on the case. My daughter is a mess, but that is to be expected when she doesn't get her way. I love you and want you to be happy. On your own terms. Call me soon. Love, Your Granny T.'"

The emotion inside me pushed out and tears ran down my cheeks as I imagined my grandmother painstakingly typing out her reassurance to me. I could picture her in her favorite chair by the window, pecking at the tiny keys with one finger as she made faces at her phone. My heart gave a little whimper at the thought. In my life, Granny T was love.

"See?" Sammy said. "Not so bad."

"They won't all be like that," I told him, sniffing. I redoubled my efforts with the pillow shield. "Mama next. Let's rip off the Band-Aid."

"Here goes: 'I can't imagine what has gotten into you, but I want you to know that a text is an unacceptable way to offer your regrets to your own wedding. By now I'm sure you have heard all my messages, and you can add 'ignoring your Mama' to the long list of social gaffes you've made in the last two days. I am humiliated. We will most likely have to leave this town. I can't imagine showing my face in public ever again.'" Sammy paused, glancing up at me, appearing to evaluate how I was holding up against this barrage.

"Go on." I swallowed down the sobs that threatened.

"'Evan is heartbroken, of course, as are his parents. And your poor Granny. She might never recover from the shame.'"

"Well, I know that's not true at least," I mumbled through the tears. I'd given up wiping them away.

"It goes on like this for about sixteen more paragraphs, Joey. Nothing new in here really. You want to hear it all?"

I shook my head. "Can you just reply 'I'm sorry, Mama. I'll call you soon.'?"

"Sure." Sammy did as I asked and sent the text.

"Let's read Daddy's and Evan's, and then I think maybe we'll call it a night?"

"Whatever you need." His voice was soft and the sympathy I heard in it almost broke me. As if I wasn't already broken.

"Okay, your daddy says: 'Sugar Pea, I need you to text me ASAP and let me know you're safe. We'll deal with everything else (aka your Mama) later, but please don't make me worry about you any more than I do already. I'm happier than ever I got you that tank to drive. Tell me you're okay, princess. I won't sleep until I know it. And then we can figure out what to do. You know I'm on your side.'"

"Oh god," I moaned, dropping my head into the pillow I was strangling. "Poor Daddy. Can you text him back real quick? Just tell him I'm fine, I'm safe with an old friend and I'll call soon?"

"Yeah," Sammy said, and now he sounded sad too. I looked up at him, hoping to understand the off note in his voice, but he looked the same as he typed in my message to Daddy.

A giggle was forming in my chest as I watched him manhandle my tiny pink sparkly phone in his big rough hands. His brow was furrowed in concentration as he bent over the device, and he looked a tiny bit like Granny T when she tried to text. But he also looked like an enormous handsome man with a tiny pink phone, and the combination of the two—and a fair amount of alcohol—made me burst out laughing.

Sammy looked up, startled. "Ah, you okay?"

I pointed at him, the laughter coming in waves I couldn't control. "It's just... It's you... and that little pink phone..."

Sammy dropped the phone to his lap in one hand, and pursed his lips. "It's your phone."

"I know," I was hysterical now, all the untapped emotion from the day coming out in uncontrollable spasms of laughter and tears at the same time. "And it's so little and sparkly..." more laughter. "And you're this huge handsome man..." now a sob escaped me. Then another laugh. A hiccup finally broke through the mess.

I was losing it. Sammy watched me a second longer, his lips lifting in a tiny smile as he picked the phone back up and finished the text to Daddy. Then he put the phone on the coffee table and rose, leaving me to be consumed by the fit of laugh-crying-hiccupping that was overtaking me. "I'm getting you some water."

The laughter was morphing into ugly crying, and I began to realize just what bad shape I was really in. I'd tossed a hand grenade blithely into the center of my life and driven away as it exploded, and now there was going to be shrapnel pretty much everywhere. And I had to clean it all up.

I didn't know how to even begin. But I knew I couldn't

just go back and step right back into that world with a demure "oops, so sorry." I couldn't put on that dress, and no matter what else I might do, I couldn't marry Evan.

Sammy returned with water, and I reached for the phone, my emotions calming enough to let me read the texts from Evan. He didn't sound angry, just hurt and confused. And I couldn't blame him.

I needed to call him and try to explain. But he deserved for me to do it when I was sober and somewhat pulled together.

"Thanks," I told Sammy, taking the water and drinking half the glass.

"You okay?" he asked. He leaned forward now, his eyebrows drawing together and his head tilted slightly as if he was trying to see deeper into me, see what was really pushing me off the deep end.

"Yeah," I put the water down and finally released the contorted throw pillow back to its proper place. "But I think the rest of these are going to have to wait. It's been a lot for one day."

He nodded, the concern never leaving his handsome face. "You should get some sleep."

It was my turn to nod, and I got to my feet, picking up the water. I looked around Sammy's house, and all the other emotions swirling inside me calmed for a moment as gratitude rose up. "Sammy?"

"Yeah?" He rose.

"Thank you. For everything."

His face broke into a smile again and he shook his head. "Always. Any time."

I stepped into his arms without thinking too much about it. I wanted the warm reassurance of his hug, one I'd enjoyed so many times when we were kids. Only, as his arms enclosed me, my body pressed flush against his warm solid chest, I realized how very different he was than the kid I'd depended on fiercely in school. This John was no kid. And this hug was every bit as reassuring and warm as they'd always been, but it was more than that.

And my muddled brain did not have room to consider what that might mean.

"Good night," I told him, stepping back.

"I'll see you in the morning, Joey. Sleep tight."

I carried my phone and my water to the guest room and shut the door, and as I drifted into an exhausted sleep, I thought about how tomorrow would be the first day of a brand new life.

CHAPTER 7
JOHN

MORE CONFUSING THAN CADE IN
A PINK SHIRT

It had been a very long and confusing day, and if you'd told me this morning that Cade Simpson sporting a pink shirt would be the least unexpected thing that would happen, I wouldn't have believed you. Cade didn't seem like a pink-wearing kind of dude, but then again, I didn't know him all that well. Still, Cade wearing a pink polo was far less surprising than Joey Baxter showing up on my doorstep.

The water heated gradually, and I waited in the privacy of my bathroom, letting the silence of the house and the sound of running water push me deeper into my own thoughts as I stood with one hand in the flow, waiting.

It was so odd to think that just a few feet away, only a couple slabs of drywall and some two-by-fours between us, slept Josephine Baxter. I had to work hard to keep myself nonchalant about the fact.

There was something undeniably nice about being needed, though it felt wrong to admit that, given the current state of my friend's life. Was it wrong to feel honored and happy that she'd chosen to come here? To me?

I knew it was, but I couldn't help it. That was how our unconventional friendship had always been. She was the popular girl, the shining blond debutante first on the list for every school dance's court, and first on the list of every guy's dream dates. And she did all that stuff. Homecoming queen, prom queen, president of student council. She fit the mold.

And yet...

She didn't.

I met Joey Baxter in fifth grade. She was blond and beautiful then too, but I was less easily swayed by such things at ten years old. It turned out what really got me interested back then was a girl who could run faster than I could. And it didn't just interest me. It pissed me off.

But there she was, in her ruffled sleeveless shirt and pink shorts, beating my ass in her white Keds and still looking perfect. It started at PE one day when we were doing those ridiculous Presidential Fitness tests. Our whole class had to do the one-mile run. It was hot—one of those swampy Alabama days when the right thing to do was to sit under a shady tree and try not to sweat. But the teacher didn't care. She filed us all by the drinking fountain and then told us to line up.

We'd been prepared for this. They sent a note home and everything. We were supposed to eat a good breakfast and come to school well hydrated.

But the night before had been one of Dad's bad nights. The kind where you stayed quiet and out of sight and just hoped the yelling and cursing would stay focused on the game. TJ and I stayed in our room while Dad screamed and drank, hoping he'd fall asleep so we could find something quick to eat for dinner while he snored away on the couch. We didn't get lucky that night, though. He came looking for someone to fight with, and even though Teej tried to protect me, I was that guy. I was always that guy.

Dad didn't hit me. But he scared the shit out of me on a regular basis, making it clear I was the problem. I was the cause of his troubles. Teej always told me it wasn't true. I knew somewhere deep down it wasn't true. But it didn't make it better. And when Dad told me to go to bed and not make another sound that might remind him of my sorry existence, I followed orders. And I got myself dressed and off to school before he woke up.

So I wasn't well fed or hydrated.

And when we ran the mile, Joey Baxter beat me by almost two minutes. She finished first in the class. Ahead of all the boys. And I finished third to last, ahead of the one kid who refused to run a single step and a girl who faked a sprained ankle in the first lap.

While I practically collapsed at the end of it, Joey glowed in the sunlight like the princess she was raised to be. A princess who came over to see if I was okay, since I was hunched on the ground trying not to throw up as my friends guffawed around me.

"Yeah, I'm fine."

"You don't look fine." Joey Baxter's blue eyes had glowed on that blistering day as she'd leaned over to get a better look at me. "I'm getting you some water, John."

She returned with a cold bottle of water, handing it to me and standing there watching as I drank it while still hunched on the ground. It was the best water I'd ever tasted.

"Thanks."

She'd smiled then, and maybe I'd been a goner from that day on. But when her eyebrows pulled together and she leaned in again, she sealed the deal. "My daddy says some people are better at running super fast for short distances than pretty fast for long ones. Sprinters, he says."

"Yeah, probably true," I agreed.

"I bet you're a sprinter."

I hadn't understood what she was doing then. A big part of me just wanted her to head on back to the group of girls she usually hung around with, leave me to my misery. But she didn't. Instead, she challenged me to a race the next day. A sprint.

That night, I slipped through the kitchen before I headed to my room for homework. I filled that plastic bottle with more water, made myself two peanut butter sandwiches, which I wrapped in paper towels, and plucked an almost black banana from the counter.

The next day, I showed up at school well-hydrated and well fed. I'd had a good night's sleep, and Dad had even made spaghetti for dinner. I'd had the second sandwich at lunch, and by the time we were set to race—during our recess after lunch—I was feeling confident. I was ready now. I'd surely be able to beat this girl.

But I didn't.

I didn't beat her that day, and I didn't beat her the next day, either.

It took me almost three months to get fast enough to beat Joey Baxter. The thing she probably still didn't know was that the training she pushed me into, the incentive she gave me without even meaning to, was what drove me to be the best once I started playing hockey. In a lot of ways, Joey was the reason I was playing for the Wombats. And so many times, when training got really tough or a game wasn't looking good, I thought back to the day I finally hit the fence at the end of the playground before she did. I thought about the way she'd smiled at me and thrown her arms around my neck and yelled, "You did it, Sammy! I knew you could!"

We quit racing after that, but we kept hanging out together at recess. We played basketball, handball, and just sat on the swings, talking. It wasn't the same kind of friendship I had with any of the boys I usually hung around with, though I'm not sure at this point if I'd call those guys friends, exactly. I didn't talk to them at all. Not about anything real.

But Joey told me about her family, about her life, which sounded like it belonged on television to my young ears. We were a study in contrasts. There was nothing about the two of us that would make you look at us together and guess it would stick. Still, it did.

In middle school, Joey invited me to her house to study, since we were both in a lot of the advanced classes together. I didn't return the favor. I couldn't imagine Joey sitting at the kitchen table in our two-bedroom house, couldn't imagine what my father would find to say to her that wouldn't humiliate me more than the truths I'd told her about my life already did.

So we went on that way. We grew up together. Adjacent. Not intertwined, exactly, but still close. She lived her life and I lived mine, but there were times she was the only one I wanted to see and there were things I knew only she would understand.

Snapped back to reality, I shut off the shower and wrapped my waist in a towel, stepping out of the steam and doing my best to banish all the memories that had decided to join me in there.

"Stay in your lane, Johnny," I whispered as I stared into the mirror at my own familiar face.

Joey would always be in my heart, but I knew she'd never be mine. I'd learned that the hard way in high school, and if there was anything that had kept me out of trouble and moving in the right direction all these years, it was that I didn't have to learn the hard lessons twice.

CHAPTER 8

JOEY

JUDGMENTAL CATS

I slept.

Like a baby, like the dead—choose your simile, but I slept well. And long. And so very comfortably I wasn't quite sure where I was when I finally awoke, the sun blazing across the daisy yellow walls of the sanctuary wherein I rested.

John's house, my fuzzy head recalled. I'd found Sammy.

The knowledge created a warm calm in my bones as I stretched out in the luxurious bed.

But then I glanced at my phone to check the time.

I'd shown up in John's life unannounced, accepted the offer of his spare room, and then slept in until two in the afternoon?

I sprang from the bed and dashed through the bathroom, then raided the Target bags I'd dropped in the corner to find something to wear. Finally, hours too late when one was a guest in someone's home, I stepped out into the hallway and made my way to the living room.

The house was silent. I stood in the center of the living room for a long moment, listening. Was Sammy still asleep? Surely not. I peered out the back patio doors but didn't see him in the yard. I glanced around once more, about to head for the kitchen, when a large blue-grey cat leapt to the back of the sofa, eyeing me suspiciously with an almost electric green gaze.

"Hello," I said, oddly uncomfortable in the cat's presence. Weren't cats mostly like furniture? Just sort of around but not really involved? I didn't know this cat, but it clearly had an opinion. About me.

"Meeee-wwwwooooollll," it said.

"Okay." I glanced around again, hoping John might materialize to translate, but he did not seem to be here. "I'm going to just... I'm going to the kitchen," I told it.

The cat jumped from the back of the couch and preceded me to the kitchen, where it leapt up onto the tiled countertop and gave me the same assessing gaze from there.

"Rooowwwwr."

"I see." I did not know how to talk to cats. I had no experience with them at all, and was a little off balance at how invested this one seemed to be in interacting with me. "Should I, uh... pet you?" I reached a hand tentatively toward the cat, who quickly lifted a paw and batted at my hand.

A clear no.

"No petting. Got it." I looked around for a food container. Maybe I could distract it. "Have you eaten?"

"Rowwr."

I moved to the refrigerator and noticed an open can of cat food. Perfect. "This?" I asked, holding it up for the cat to see.

"RRRooollllwwr."

"Uh, okay. How much do you eat?" I peered into the little can, which was half gone, and then found a plate in the cabinet and dumped the food onto it. "Okay. Here. Friends?" I placed the plate in front of the cat, who continued staring at me for a moment longer than I thought was strictly necessary to say thank you, and then it tucked into its feast.

Good. Okay. That was handled. But feeding the cat made me realize how hungry I was. I found myself a glass and poured water, and then turned to glance at the cat again. It had risen to all fours to eat, and now I saw that there was a note beneath its paws, which it had been sitting on a moment ago.

I sidled nearer, slowly reaching out a hand to pull the note from beneath the cat. It paused, watching me retrieve the paper, but didn't complain.

Joey,

I had to go work out for a bit and then get a little time on the ice. I'll be back by four. There's plenty of stuff in the fridge if you're hungry. I hope you slept well.

 - John

. . .

It was a relief to find the note, though I felt a strange pang of disappointment that John wasn't here. I'd been looking forward to seeing him, I realized.

There was a good selection of food in the refrigerator. Boxes upon boxes of prepared chicken and diced sweet potatoes, broccoli and quinoa. John was evidently a healthy eater. I could roll with that.

I made myself a plate, heated it in the microwave, and took it to the kitchen table.

The cat licked its plate and then seemed happy enough to accept my presence in the kitchen. It jumped down from the counter and disappeared once again.

Weird. I wouldn't have thought of John as a cat guy.

When I was done eating, I had no further excuses. I needed to listen to the messages on my phone and decide what I was going to do with my life.

My mother's were predictable. My father's were reassuring. Those left by my friends were borderline hysterical, but I knew that was only because me leaving my own wedding in the dust was the most exciting thing that had happened in Peach Tree Grove in ages. It was Evan's messages that kind of broke my heart.

"Babe, I just don't get it. Weren't we happy? Didn't we have everything we wanted?"

We did. Or at least he did. And I'd really thought maybe it would be enough.

"Honey, I'm not mad. I just want to understand. What's so tough that you couldn't talk to me about it first?"

I knew he was right. A real couple—a strong couple, the kind that should be getting married—would be able to talk about anything.

"Joey, come on. At least let me know when you want to reschedule all this. I'm gonna have to rearrange a few things at the firm. This is pretty inconvenient, but I'm not mad, babe. Just lemme know when you think you'll be ready."

It was his last message that had me finally dialing his number.

He didn't understand. But I could barely remember what I'd told him as I'd driven out of town. He deserved a real explanation. And for heaven's sake, he needed to know I wasn't going to be rescheduling anything. I swallowed a bit of fear as I held my phone, reminding myself that I'd done the right thing. For me, and for him too.

"Babe? Hi. You okay?" Evan's voice was familiar and worried, and it softened my resolve a bit, but I knew I could care about him without him being the man I was meant to marry. "Tell me you're okay, baby."

"I'm okay. I'm at a friend's place in Virginia." My voice was steadier than I'd expected.

"Okay," he said, and I could hear him breathing deeply. I pictured him pinching the bridge of his nose like he often did when he was trying to think deeply or control his emotions. "Tell me what's going on."

My heart pulsed with guilt and pain and regret—not at what I'd done, but at how it had affected everyone else. "I just... Oh Evan, I'm really sorry. I should have told you this a long time ago."

"Is there someone else?"

Surprise rippled through me. "No! Of course not."

"Then why would you leave like this? I don't understand."

"I know. I'm so sorry."

"Joey, listen, everyone gets cold feet. Totally normal. I mean, not everyone jumps in the car and drives five states away, but..." a mirthless laugh came through the phone. "Just... let's get this done, okay?"

"Get this done?" I asked, surprise pushing my spine straighter as I sat staring into John's backyard. "Get married, you mean?"

"Yeah. I mean, the whole schedule's shot, a lot of money burnt. But we can salvage some of it. Your mama's pretty mad, but she'll get over it. Just get back down here and let's figure it out."

I waited, but Evan didn't say anything about loving me, about wanting to spend his life with me. He went on more about schedules and money, and I began to realize that maybe he wasn't getting married for the right reasons either.

"Ev?" I said, interrupting his one-sided discussion of potential future dates.

"Yeah?" His voice was tense. Irritated.

"Do you really love me? You really wanted me to be your wife? Like...forever?"

"Joey..." he drew out my name like the question had exhausted him. "Where is this coming from?"

"Do you love me?" I asked again.

"Of course." There was no conviction in his words.

"But is it the kind of thing you don't think you can survive without? Is it like drinking water for the first time?" John's words rang through my head.

"What? Water? Joey, what are you talking about?"

I swallowed hard, gathering my resolve. "I don't think we love each other enough to get married, Evan. I think we like each other a lot and respect each other, and most of all that we're just comfortable because we've known each other a long time and our families are friends." He didn't interrupt, so I went on. "But I've done puzzles where they were lazy cutting the pieces."

"Joey—I'm at work since we're not on our honeymoon like we planned... I don't have time to chat about puzzles. I can talk with you later, but I assure you, darlin, you're the one I want to be my wife."

The way he said that made it sound like he'd chosen me off a shelf of many suitable potential wives. It was like a door snapping shut, and suddenly I had zero doubt I'd done the right thing. I continued.

"Sometimes there are lots of pieces that fit but none that are actually right." My voice trailed off as I finished my stupid puzzle analogy.

"Oh. Okay. Well, I think you're the right fit."

"I don't think I am."

"Jo..."

"Evan, I'm not going to marry you. And I want you to find someone you really love. Someone you can't live without. I'm not her, don't you see that?"

"I... No, we..." Evan was finally getting the message.

"I'm sorry. I should've done this a long time ago. I really

am sorry, Evan. Please apologize to your mama for me." I ended the call, hoping Evan wasn't too upset. One thing reassured me though—I didn't think he was heartbroken, just inconvenienced and maybe embarrassed.

I took a deep breath and held the phone out again to call my mother. I squeezed my eyes shut and tried to prepare for the barrage I knew I'd be inviting. She'd be angry. She'd twist my words and try to change my mind. She was a master of guilt. I needed to be ready.

"Josephine." Mama's voice was calm, reserved. That tone hid a dangerous storm beneath it. It was the voice she'd used when I'd done something grievous as a child and it had the same effect on me now as it did back then. Cold water raced through my bloodstream.

"Hi Mama."

"You've made a perfect mess of everything here. It would have been less devastating if you'd just set the house on fire."

Mama had a gift for exaggeration, though I didn't doubt I'd essentially burned an awful amount of money and time by running away.

"I know, Mama. I'm sorry. I wasn't thinking clearly, but I am now. And Mama? I can't marry him."

"Of course you can. He's perfect, and if he's willing to forgive this mess we might even convince a few people to attend the ceremony to see it."

The image those words conveyed sent a shudder through me. "No."

"No? What exactly are you refusing, Josephine? No, you don't want the perfect life I've helped you arrange? No, you don't want your daddy and I to have the satisfaction of knowing you'll be well taken care of? No, you don't want to give your friends and relatives the pleasure of watching you marry a man who is ideal?"

"No, I am not going to marry Evan."

Mama blew out a breath as if I was just a child having a tantrum that would soon pass.

"I mean it, Mama. I'm really sorry, but—"

"Just come back home. We'll talk here."

"I think I might not come back right away." I hadn't discussed this with John, but I could find somewhere else to stay if I had to. I couldn't go back.

"Don't be ridiculous. There's nothing for you there... where even are you?"

"Virginia."

"Why in the world are you in Virginia? Where are you sleeping?"

"With John."

Mama's sharp inhale confirmed that did not come out quite right.

"I mean, at John's house. Not with John," I amended my statement as quickly as I could.

"Who is John?" Mama sounded scandalized as she hissed this question.

"You remember him. From school. John Samuels."

"The skinny little boy from the flats?" The outskirts of Peach Tree Grove were called "the flats," and to anyone who lived in the town proper, it was like saying "the slums."

Still, that was how she thought of John Samuels because

his life growing up had been very different from mine. "Yes. Only, he's grown up too now."

"Well you can't stay with him, that'll certainly cause a scandal, as if your fleeing your own wedding wasn't enough. You'll come back immediately, and we'll get to work rebooking the caterer. I suspect I can negotiate a discount of some kind, though we may have to accept a Friday evening or a Sunday affair. I'm sure Saturdays are booked through the next year." The idea of rebooking my wedding date sounded like it exhausted my mother.

It exhausted me, but having yet another conversation where the person on the other end did not seem to think I had any idea what I was doing with my own life had lit a little fire inside me that was beginning to grow.

"Mama. You're not listening to me. I'm not coming back. Not right now. And I'm not marrying Evan."

"Don't be—"

"I am not being ridiculous. I'm being an adult. I am taking responsibility for my own life, and I will not marry someone I don't love. I need some time to figure out who I really am and what I want for my life. But being Mrs. Evan Stratton in Peach Tree Grove isn't it."

"Josephine." Mama's voice was low, filled with menace. "Do you have any idea what you're saying?"

"I do. I'm saying I need to be in charge of my own life. I appreciate all you and Daddy have done for me, and I'm very sorry for the way things turned out with the wedding—"

"Have you any idea the expense your father went to?"

"I know, and—"

"You can stay there," Mama said, her voice never losing that glinting, devastating edge. "But you will not be enjoying another dime of your father's assistance. I'll ensure your credit card is closed immediately."

I'd known it would happen, but it would make things a bit harder. "I understand."

Perhaps Mama had thought the threat of being cut off would bring me back, because this seemed to surprise her.

"No money. No support from us," she explained.

"That's only fair. Thank you for understanding, Mama. I'll call again soon. I love you." I ended the call before I had to hear again what a disappointment I was, my head falling into my arms on John's kitchen table. For a few moments, I let myself cry, the misery at having just let my family down and gotten myself cut off rolling through me and washing out with my tears. When I raised my head again to find the cat sitting on the other end of the table watching me with that assessing green stare, I felt lighter. Renewed.

I had nothing. But it was better somehow than all the heavy things I'd been saddled with back at home.

When I stood up and tucked my phone into my jeans pocket I felt a little bit unmoored, like my life had suddenly been detached from all its protective bindings and I was floating freely for the first time. It was surprising how easy it had been to sort through the devastation I'd wrought. For some reason I'd expected to be on the phone for hours, to have my soul pulled free of my body and run through a paper shredder, and to be left with unidentifiable bits of myself requiring reassembly. But I didn't feel disassembled at all. I felt new.

But being suddenly new and disconnected was frightening too. Where was I supposed to go from here? I tried to pull at some long-neglected threads of determination within me, but I couldn't seem to grasp them. It had been a long time since I'd needed to rely on myself—was I even capable of it now?

I stepped out into the warmth of the backyard and let my mind work through some options. I could go home. But no, that was not a real option. I'd walk right back into the cage I'd just escaped from. Could I go back to Alabama and just be clear that I was going to be a single girl, making my own way? It would be awfully difficult to be that close to home and not get lured back in—or hurt, if my family decided to keep me at arm's length. So then, somewhere else. For now, here, I guessed. If John would have me for a bit. But I'd need a real plan.

I was exploring the back yard and trying to keep a brave face on when I heard John's truck pulling into the garage, and I waited just outside, eager to tell him how much better things already seemed—maybe I could convince myself while I was at it. Only, when he came through the glass door to join me on the patio, his face suggested we'd be having a different conversation altogether.

CHAPTER 9
JOHN

NO PLAN SHOULD INVOLVE
GETTING UP BEFORE NINE

It was strange coming home to find Joey there, waiting for me.

She greeted me with an uncertain smile, standing just outside the living room on the patio.

In one way, it was glorious, like something I'd imagined coming to life. The sun caught strands of burnished gold in her loose blond hair, and the faded jeans she wore hung loose beneath the sleeveless T-shirt, giving her a casual, comfortable look that made me want to scoop her into my arms and hug her. But the expression on her face--the soft wide smile, the bright enthusiastic eyes—made me realize I might not be up to her optimism today.

"Hey Joey," I said, stepping out to join her and collapsing onto the couch in the shade.

"How was training?" She joined me on the couch, practically glowing, the way I remembered from when we were younger. Something had shifted with her—she didn't look worried or upset.

"You look good. Happy? Everything okay at home?"

She lifted a shoulder and pushed her hair back over it, the single casual move drawing my eye, giving me distant thoughts of what it would be like to run my hands through that hair, touch that golden skin. "Everything will be okay. I got cut off, as predicted."

"Your dad pretty mad?"

"I doubt it, but my mother's still upset."

"That tracks." Joey's mother got upset about all kinds of things when we were kids. Grass stains on the knees of pants, eating cookies without a plate and napkin, actual people in the sitting room, which was clearly never used for sitting or anything else.

"She'll get over it. Maybe."

"So you got a chance to talk to her?"

Joey nodded, her eyes never leaving my face, like she was trying to figure something out. "Sammy? What's wrong?"

She'd always been able to read me. No matter how I tried to play off whatever feelings I had at any point in time, she always saw through it. "Nah, everything's good. Just worried about keeping up for the team." That was an understatement. Ever since Mizzoni had left, I'd been having nightmares about losing everything, about everyone figuring out I was a fraud.

"You wouldn't be where you are if you couldn't keep up," Joey said.

Joey was a friend, saying what was expected. But she didn't know anything about hockey, about the pressure I was under. This wasn't a conversation we needed to have.

This was my issue to work through. "Yeah, I'm sure you're right. Just a rough workout today." I forced my shoulders down, shook out my hands. "You got a good night's sleep?"

She laughed, the rays of late afternoon sunshine appearing to dance and shift along with her voice. "I guess I needed it."

I wanted to ask her about her plans, her expectations here. But I didn't want to be one more person pushing her for answers. Still, there was a part of me that thought it'd be easier to focus on hockey and getting myself ready for next season if she wasn't here too long. At the same time, I didn't want to say goodbye to her, either. My head was almost as much a mess as my workout had been today.

"Well, I'm not sure what your plans are for the rest of the day," I began, but Joey was laughing again, the bright crystalline sound easing some of my own darkness.

"I have zero plans, Sammy. I'm just here. Existing. I need to figure some stuff out for sure."

"Okay, well, maybe short-term plans? Food?"

"I just had lunch, but in a little bit, yeah."

"I've gotta clean up a little anyway. You feel like getting out again? Or dinner here?"

"How about this... you go do what you need to do but point me to a grocery store first. I'll cook."

I felt my eyebrows go up. I needed to be careful about what I ate, but Joey offering to cook was a whole other thing. My mind flashed back to the nights I'd stayed at her house for dinner. Dad could cook canned spaghetti, but her family ate like royalty. My mouth watered at the thought of it. "I can't really say no to that," I admitted.

Joey scrunched her nose and smiled at me. "Why would you say no?"

She was right. I couldn't imagine ever saying no to her. "I wouldn't. But I would tell you that I'm supposed to be staying in shape, so maybe we try to stick to the lighter side of things?"

"I don't even know what that means!" Joey laughed and stood, and I put the name of the grocery store into her mapping app and then headed back toward the shower.

"John?" she called just before I disappeared through the door.

"Yeah?"

"What's your cat's name?"

"That's Hank. It's his house. I think it's more that I'm his person than that he's my cat. He was here first." I could picture Joey's confused face at this explanation, and a little laugh escaped me as she said, "Oh. Okay."

I closed my door to shower and took a long hot one. When I opened the door again, Joey was back, and I could hear her moving around in the kitchen while she sang along to Luke Combs. I followed the sounds of "Fast Car" out to find Joey dancing in front of the stove while Hank sat behind her on the counter, watching intently.

Joey moved gracefully—of course. Everything she did was graceful, even when she'd kicked my ass at running. Her hips swayed and her shoulders moved, and she looked so happy here in my house, so right, it made my heart squeeze for no reason at all.

I offered to help, but she shooed me away, so I sat down at the little table by the window while Joey cooked, and though I glanced at my phone a few times, mostly I just sat and let the scene move around me. Joey looked totally at ease in my house, and I felt more calm and centered than I had in a while, just sitting here, being with her.

Before long, the smells wafting around had my stomach growling and I offered to set the table and Joey gave me a smile that made me warm and shivery all at once.

"That'd be great. Almost ready here."

I laid out the silverware and napkins, and then poured us each a glass of water.

"Do you want a glass of wine with dinner?" I asked her.

"No thanks," she said, smiling at me again and making me practically forget what I'd just asked her. Having her here was taking more getting used to than I'd expected.

Soon, we were sitting across from one another, a plate of smothered pork chops and greens in front of me and snatches of our childhood flickering through my head.

"This your mother's recipe?" I asked hopefully. Mrs. Baxter had never seemed to be my biggest fan, but it hadn't kept her from glowing when I ate the food she made like it was the best thing I'd ever had. Because it was.

"It is," Joey confirmed. "I remembered that you always liked it."

"I liked everything your mother made," I told her. It was true. The Baxter's kitchen was like a factory in constant production. There was always a cake under glass on the counter, or a plate of cookies somewhere nearby, something simmering on the stove or baking in the oven, dishes drying next to the sink. It was a sharp contrast to the cold, quiet of my own house, where Dad would stumble in somewhere after five each night and rummage through the refrigerator in hopes of finding a meal he forgot was in there. Our kitchen was cans and freezer trays, empty glasses abandoned in the sink, while Joey's kitchen was pots and pans, warm smells and people.

As I shoveled another bite into my mouth I looked up at Joey, across from me. Her skin glowed and when she caught me watching her, her full pink lips pulled up into a little smile. But she wasn't eating much.

"Thanks for this," I said.

"It's the least I could do." Her tanned shoulder lifted and dropped.

"You're not hungry?" I watched her push a piece of pork chop around her plate and then lay her fork down.

"I guess not, not really."

I watched her as she avoided my eyes, realizing that her brightness and cheer earlier might just have been an act. Of course they were. She'd run away—exploded her own life plan. It would be unlikely that she'd be over that already.

"How are you really doing?" I asked her, pushing aside my own bad day for a minute. What did I really have to complain about, anyway?

She lifted her gaze to mine, those thick lashes fluttering up and down, and then she dropped her eyes to her lap. "I'll be okay. I'm just... I'm trying to figure out what I'm supposed to do now, I guess." She sighed after she said this, and my heart squeezed, wishing I could bring the dancing, smiling version of my friend back.

"That makes sense. Everything in your life changed pretty quick there."

"And I didn't really have a plan for what I'd do next," she said. When she lifted her gaze again, the big blue eyes I loved were shining and sad. "I'm so naive, aren't I? My parents are right."

I dropped my own fork. "You're not naive. And you can't take your parents at face value right now. They're just upset."

She leaned back in her chair, lifting a hand to trace the line of condensation down her water glass. "No, they've told me I was naive long before I exploded my wedding."

"Why?"

She let out a little laugh, but there was no joy in it and my insides recoiled at the misery of the sound. "I'm just a daddy's girl, I guess. Can't do much for myself."

"You don't believe that." I almost hissed the words. This wasn't the Joey I grew up with. That girl had the world in her hand, believed she could do anything—and she could.

"Let's consider," she said, and I didn't like the cold flat tone of her voice. "I got engaged in my third year of school and then moved back into my daddy's house. My only real plan was to be Evan's wife. To cook dinners and entertain guests, maybe join the junior league or the Peach Tree Grove women's club and raise money for charity. And now? I can't even do that."

"Is that what you wanted to do?"

She held my gaze, but her eyes narrowed slightly as her head tilted to one side. "That's the thing..."

I waited, wondering what the thing could be. The thing that had changed my headstrong and capable best friend into exactly the girl she always told me she didn't want to be.

"I guess at some point after you and I headed off to find our futures, I lost sight of what I wanted to do. And now? Now, I just don't know."

I shook my head. Maybe she just needed me to remind her who she was. "The Joey I knew had the world on a string. She had plans. You were going to be a genetic scientist. You were going to help cure cancer."

She laughed, the sound reminding me of the way an adult might laugh when a toddler declared that they would be an astronaut or a princess. She laughed like it was a far-fetched idea. Or worse—Impossible.

"You've got your degree, right?"

Her eyes flicked to mine, then dropped again. "I do."

"In what?" I braced myself, expecting her mother might have talked her into pursuing something practical, like housekeeping. Did they offer degrees in that?

"Biological and biomedical science."

Excitement replaced the foreboding. She was still in there. She'd stuck to her guns. "That's great, Joey."

She eyed me again, and her expression told me it wasn't maybe as great as I thought.

"It would be, if I'd been working in the field. Right now, it's just a useless piece of paper."

"Joey, you're twenty-three, not seventy-five. Life's not over."

"Everyone I graduated with had job offers."

That sounded like good news. "Amazing."

"Based on the years of interning they did while we were in school."

"Makes sense."

"I didn't intern."

"Okay, but you could start now, right?"

She shook her head sadly. "I doubt it. I've spent years doing nothing while my peers gained valuable experience. I'm behind. I wouldn't even know where to start now."

I shook my head. "You're not behind, Joey." Where had the optimism and sunshine vanished to? This Joey was a shadow of the girl I used to know.

My friend hit me with a smile that just about cracked my heart in pieces. It was her mother's smile, one that came from training and manners, not the bright sunshine smile that I loved, the one that came from somewhere deep inside her heart. "Sometimes it just feels that way, I guess." She shook her head lightly as if scattering any dark thoughts. "I'll be fine, John. Either way, it's definitely nothing for you to worry about. I'm just realizing that maybe I should have thought a little harder about what came next instead of just running away."

Joey rose and collected our plates, and I did the same, helping her clean up the kitchen. But there was a cool silence between us, and I knew it was borne of her second-guessing herself. I didn't like it.

Whether she had a plan or not, Joey had made the right move breaking away from an early marriage and a life spent as someone's obedient trophy wife. I just had to figure out how to make her see it, make her see herself the way she had when she'd beat my ass time and again running for the fence on the playground.

It was still early when we'd finished cleaning the kitchen, but Joey turned to me, that sad expression still in her eyes.

"I'm going to go to bed early, Sammy. See if I can get up at a decent hour." She stepped close to hug me.

My arms went around her, and I tried to ignore the warmth of her body pressed to mine, the swell of her breasts against my chest. I tried to ignore the way my blood surged and my mind tried to short-circuit as the scent of her hair wound through my senses. She didn't need any of that from me. She needed me to be her friend, and that's what I'd be.

But I'd have to cut this hug short, or she'd feel the evidence of my less-than-friendly notions against her hip in a moment. I stepped back, breaking the contact, and my brain began functioning again.

"I have an idea," I told her.

Those big blue eyes met mine and the idea got bigger. I was going to banish that sadness. I was going to find Joey in there again. More importantly, I was going to show her that nothing had changed. She was still the firecracker of a girl who trusted herself and made those around her do the same.

"Be up at seven," I said.

"Seven?" she looked almost offended at the idea of that early hour.

"Seven."

CHAPTER 10
JOEY

NO. I DON'T... GYM.

Sleep didn't come right away.

That burst of energy I'd had after wrapping up my phone calls had slowly faded, leaving behind a wake of dreary self-doubt and second guesses. What had I done? And why hadn't I bothered to think it through?

I tossed and turned, replaying my mother's voice in my head.

It wasn't so much that they had cut me off. I mean, yes, money was something I was used to. Something I would need at some point soon when my cash ran out. But it was more than that. It was the feeling that if I didn't conform to Mama's expectations, then I wasn't worth her effort. The notion that if I strayed from the cushioned and well-tread path she'd set me on, I'd get no support from her—financial or otherwise.

I hoped she was just hurt. And maybe Daddy would help her come around a bit. But before I could expect anything like that, I had to figure out what exactly I was asking them to accept. Who was I now? Who would I become?

I'd been shaped and formed for such a long time I didn't have any real idea. And worse? I felt weak. Powerless. I'd exerted all the power I had in running away. Now? I had nothing.

I was awakened by an obnoxious and very loud whirring sound. Mechanical. A lawnmower?

I glanced at my phone. It wasn't even seven yet. Who was mowing their lawn at this hour? And why did it sound like they were in John's kitchen?

Moving clumsily from the soft, cozy bed, I cracked the bedroom door open. Louder. The noise was definitely coming from inside the house.

"Rooowwwwllllr." Hank sat just outside my door.

"Hello," I told him.

He seemed to see that as an invitation, and he pushed past me into the room, winding his way past my sock-clad feet to leap up onto the bed and judge me from there.

"What?" I asked, shutting the door again. "Did that noise wake you up too?"

Hank just watched me, saying nothing.

Cats.

"I'm going in the bathroom. You'll have to stay out here. Staring in there would just be rude. And weird."

I closed myself in the little bathroom and stared into the

mirror for a minute, trying to see if I looked different somehow. If my exterior matched my suddenly discombobulated interior.

Besides smeared eye makeup and a sleep crease along one side of my cheek, the answer was no. I splashed water on my face and tugged my hair into a ponytail, did the other required business, and stepped back out into the bedroom to slip on some clothes. Hank was nowhere in sight, which was strange, because I didn't see how he could have left the room with the door shut.

With a sigh, I pulled the door open again and was about to step out when the cat brushed past me in a hurry, having appeared from nowhere.

Cats.

I stumbled toward the brightly lit kitchen, and identified the source of the noise. John was pouring something bright orange from the top part of a blender into two tall glasses.

"Smoothie?" I asked.

"Protein, some healthy fat. Some fruit. You'll need it."

I accepted the glass he held out and looked at him over the rim. His handsome face was clean shaven, and his hair slicked back. He wore a sleeveless workout shirt and a pair of athletic shorts, and if I hadn't been so sleepy, I certainly would have managed some admiration for that. His arms did not need sleeves, that was for sure. They were better bare so a person could admire all the various muscles. If a person was so inclined.

"Why exactly will I need this?" I sipped the smoothie. It was delicious, if a little over-healthy tasting. I liked bacon in the morning. This was not bacon.

"You'll need the energy."

I felt myself frown. Energy was one thing I did not feel like I had a whole lot of at the present time, and not just because it was so early.

John saved me from asking more questions. "I'm taking you to the gym."

"Ew. No. I don't... gym." Visions of sweaty muscle heads filled my mind. "I belong to a yoga studio at home."

Home. What a strange word.

"I mean I did. In Peach Tree Grove..." My statement dwindled with my desire to speak at all. Yoga, like everything else, was part of my life before. Which I'd abandoned. Suddenly. Without thinking through the long-term consequences. Like no longer belonging to the fancy yoga studio I loved.

"Yoga's great. We can do that here too," John said, tipping a finger to the bottom edge of the glass forgotten in my hand as if encouraging me to drink more. I obeyed. "But I have the sense you need to do something a bit more intense."

What? Why? John was speaking another language suddenly. Where was this coming from? "Intense? Like kickboxing?"

"We'll start with weights and go from there."

I shook my head. "I don't think I want to lift weights." I'd lifted weights before. Small ones. In organized classes with lots of other ladies who had small weights to lift too. It just wasn't something I had experience with. Weight lifting —real weightlifting—was for athletes and bodybuilders. Also... "John," I ventured, narrowing my eyes at him and sucking in my stomach. "Are you suggesting I need to lose weight?"

John's eyes flew open and his free hand went up in front of him, palm toward me. "No, no. Nothing like that." He adopted the appropriately apologetic tone of a man caught commenting on a woman's size. "That's not what I'm saying at all. Like, at all."

I sipped my smoothie, still eyeing him. "So what, then?"

"This is about how you feel inside. Not how you look outside. Outside you look..." John paused, a blush climbing into his cheeks suddenly. "Ah, I mean, you know how you look. You're perfect."

I gave him a second to struggle with his discomfort, enjoying it a bit more than I probably should have. "Perfect, huh?" I swayed from one foot to the other. Even if superficial compliments changed very little about my current predicament, I liked the idea that John thought I looked good. "So we're going to go work out my insides with weights."

"Something like that," John said, clearly relieved to be back on safe ground. "Do you have anything else to wear?" He eyeballed my capri pants and sleeveless top. "Shorts?"

"You saw what I got at Target," I reminded him.

He nodded. "Leggings maybe?"

"I have leggings. And a long tee."

"Perfect." He grinned widely at me, and I had the distinct impression he was summoning up extra enthusiasm to make up for my total lack.

"I guess I'll go change," I said, not finding the energy to even feign excitement for John's plan.

He must've heard it in my voice, because he called after me, "you'll like this. I promise."

"Don't make promises you can't keep, Sammy."

The gym John took me to was a sprawling industrial space filled with machines, weight racks, and people of all shapes and sizes working intently at various pursuits.

"I'll head over there," I told him, pointing to a row of treadmills where the occupants wore headphones and all seemed to be watching home improvement shows on the built-in TVs. I could zone out and stroll for an hour while John did whatever he needed to do.

"I don't think so," John said, catching my arm and tugging me back to his side. "We'll do a functional warm up and then we're lifting."

I cast another envious gaze at the people left to their own devices on the cardio machines and followed John to an open spot on the floor near a couple benches and a lot of free weights lined up along a mirror. There were a few men around, most of them large and sweaty, and none of them paying any attention to us. Or at least to me.

"How's it going, Samuels?" one of them asked as he dropped a set of enormous dumbbells back onto the rack.

"Good, Foster. How are you? How's the family?"

The man's face broke into a friendly smile. "Great. Twins are a lot though."

"You get time to escape," John pointed out.

"Mental health is important." Foster's eyes drifted past John and found me for a brief second, and he gave me a little smile. "Hey, enjoy your workout," he told us both, turning back to the rack.

"You too, man." John gave me a smile and turned to the benches on the floor. He moved a couple out of the way and then looked at me. "You stand here. Just do what I do. We're going to move through some exercises to get our muscles ready to work."

"Aren't you supposed to be doing this kind of thing with your team? Like, don't you have a bunch of fancy facilities and stuff?"

"I do go there sometimes," John answered, his face growing solemn. "But I like to work out on my own too." I sensed he was not going to add more to that, so I nodded my acceptance and filed away a thought to ask him more about the team later. Seemed like something was up.

I watched as John reached up over his head and then folded in half. Easy. I could do that. I did the same, feeling the stretch through my back. Stretching was good. I should remember to do more of it. Then he dropped his palms to the floor and walked his hands out until his body was straight, balanced between his hands and feet. Harder, but I could do it. I followed suit.

Next, John lowered himself, his chest almost touching the ground. Eh. Okay. I did the same, my arms feeling shaky.

John pushed himself back up. I flailed, but managed it after lowering a knee.

"Down dog," he said, pushing back with his hands into the familiar yoga post.

"I know this one," I said, happy to be back on familiar ground. I pushed my hips into the air and let my head hang between my hands. I didn't know about weights or going to the gym, but John had been right—moving felt good.

He walked his hands back between his feet and then rolled slowly back up to standing, and I did the same and gave him a grin in the mirror.

"We done now?" I knew we weren't, but I'd found my stride playing the resistant student and I wasn't going to quit yet.

"Not even close. Take a deep breath and let's do that about ten more times."

"Meh." I followed John through the movements, my body warming and loosening with each repetition. The pushup was the hard part, and I managed a couple that I thought were pretty good, but I didn't like how weak I felt in that position. Surely, I should be able to lift my own body weight, but I could not.

When we were done, my breath came a little harder, and I could feel my blood moving. Even though I'd be happy to stop and go get a mocha latte instead, there was something about moving that felt intrinsic, like this was what my body was supposed to be doing. It had been a while since I'd had that feeling.

"Today we'll focus on chest and a little bit of legs," John said, glancing around the gym, appearing to take stock.

"You want to focus on my chest, huh?" I teased.

John blushed, but managed to ignore it. "Those pushups looked a little rough."

"They were."

For the next forty-five minutes, John led me around the weight floor, sitting me on equipment, handing me weights, and directing me. He corrected my form frequently, which was no surprise since this was the first time I'd done any of these movements. But he did it in the same friendly and encouraging way he did everything.

"Keep your elbows at ninety degrees," he said, kneeling behind me as I lay on a bench with a dumbbell in each hand. I lowered the weight carefully, my arms shaking a little, and my elbows landed in John's warm palms. "Right there," he said. "No lower than that, okay?"

I gathered my strength and pressed the dumbbells back up, feeling John's reassuring presence just behind me the whole time. He showed me how to use my legs to lower the weights without hurting myself, his hands brushing and pressing my arms, my legs, my back—all of it in the name of guiding me and correcting my form. The gentle touches were having a few other effects on me too, namely forcing me to notice how warm and rough his hands were, how carefully he touched me, how hot he looked when he was concentrating.

But none of that was what this was about. John wasn't here for me to transfer my desperate need for purpose onto him. I'd barely ended a serious relationship, anyway. These were probably just some kind of chemical rebound urges. Only... I'd never had thoughts like this about Evan. Ever.

"You doing okay?" John asked as we finished the last set

of incline chest press.

"Tired," I said, taking stock of my body in a way I hadn't done in a while. "A little shaky, I guess." I glanced around. I'd felt self-conscious when we'd begun, but all the other people here seemed focused entirely on their own work-outs. Except for a couple friendly nods and hellos, they'd left us alone.

"That's what you want to feel," John said, putting our weights back and wiping them down. "You're stressing and tearing muscle fibers, and now we'll work on nutrition and rest to help them grow back stronger."

I looked at the very pronounced muscles on John's arms, and traced one finger lightly over the swell of his shoulder tapering into the biceps and down to the muscled forearm. "These are nice on you," I told him, dropping my hand and meeting his startled eyes. "But I'm not really looking for the gainz, I don't think."

Those dark eyes crinkled at the corners as he laughed. "Don't worry about that. You're not going to get huge any time soon. And most women just aren't built to put on tons of muscle without really trying to achieve that look."

"You saying I'm weak?" I challenged, grinning.

"I'm saying you're stronger than you realize and I'm going to help you remember it."

Well. I hadn't expected that answer. I wasn't quite sure what he meant, or what strength John thought I had. It had been a long time since I'd felt anything like strong. I didn't have a snappy comeback, so I sucked down some water and then followed John to the little cafe counter at the front of the gym.

"Protein," he said. "And whatever else sounds good."

I gazed up at the menu, which was full of bowls and shakes and all kinds of add-ins and confusing supplements. Then I spotted it. "Can I have the coffee shake?"

"One coffee and one banana-peanut butter shake, please," John told the teenage boy behind the counter.

"Coming right up," he said, turning away. He went about his business, mixing up ingredients and running blenders, but he glanced at John as we waited. "You're the goalie, right? For the Wombats?"

I loved watching John react. He dropped the kid's eyes for a second and one hand went to the back of his neck as he looked back up and nodded with a smile. Bashful, but proud. "Yeah, I am."

"Dude, you're incredible. We can't wait to see what you do this season."

"Well, that makes two of us," John told him. "Thanks." He paid for the shakes and we headed outside.

"Thanks for this," I said, lifting my cup towards him. "And for the workout."

John didn't say anything, but we walked to his truck, and he popped the locks, throwing his bag inside. He looked at me across the front seat, since I'd just pulled open the passenger side door. "Want to go sit in the park for a second while we finish these?" He angled his head at the green space next to the gym, where trees bloomed with leaves and blossoms, and kids ran with dogs around the little central playground.

"Sure," I agreed. It was a beautiful sunny day—a little warm, but nothing like Alabama.

We headed for the park and found a shady bench, the summer air wafting gently around us in a magnolia-scented breeze.

"So," I said, letting my eyes rest on the stumbling strides of a toddler crossing the sandbox carrying a toy truck to another kid. "Why do you work out at a different gym than your teammates?"

For a moment, I didn't think John was going to answer me. But then he said, "It's complicated."

I turned to look at him, studying the way his smooth forehead tucked into those dark expressive brows, his proud nose jutting out just above soft, full lips. He had a very nice profile—and besides the fact he was handsome, there was also a lot about looking at him that made me feel calm and centered. John was my past, my happy place. It was why I'd come to him when my world was falling apart. And now? He looked like maybe he needed a happy place of his own.

"Tell me," I pushed.

He took a long pull from his straw, making his Adam's apple bob in a very distracting way, and then lowered the cup and gave me a little smile that didn't look happy at all. "I have a lot to prove to those guys, is all. To everyone, really."

I waited because that didn't begin to answer my question or explain why he sounded so tormented.

"I told you before that I'm the youngest starting goalie in the FHL," he went on finally. "And while I'm glad to be that guy, it's a lot of pressure."

"Okay," I said, still not understanding the origin of what

felt like a deep-seated worry somewhere in that heavy gaze.

"It's just... I'm not sure I'm ready for it. And so I throw in some extra workouts. The rest of the guys are just holding their spots, right? The spots they earned and contracted for. But I got pushed into mine before anyone was really expecting me to be there, least of all me."

"Why?"

"Because Mizzoni wasn't supposed to leave yet. I was supposed to have at least a year to learn from him, to grow. Instead, I ended up being first string at the end of last season, and I barely held it together."

"You're worried you're not qualified?" That seemed unlikely. John had been a hockey prodigy since he'd started playing in junior high, and no one worked harder than he did.

"I know I'm not."

I felt my mouth drop open. I snapped it shut. "Of course you are. They don't go drafting just anyone and hoping it works out. You climbed a very rough ladder to prove you belong right where you are."

John let out a sigh, rubbing a hand through his hair and tipping his head back to stare up at the crystal blue sky through the branches of the tree under which we sat.

"Are you supposed to do extra practices in the off season? Don't they worry about you getting hurt?"

He rolled his head to squint at me. "Maybe."

"I see." John was suffering from imposter syndrome. He didn't think he deserved to be where he was. And I knew why. "Well, I hope you'll forgive me for saying so, but your dad is a dick, by the way."

A laugh sputtered from John's lips and he sat back up, smiling at me. "Where did that come from?"

I sniffed. "I saw it when we were kids, and I'm guessing he's the one making you feel this way now." John's father had come to pick him up from my house a few times, and I'd met him at school as a kid. He'd also joined our family for dinner once at my father's invitation. That had not gone especially well. The man had spent the meal telling my parents how fantastic his other son TJ was at football. While John sat beside him.

"He's okay. This isn't about him."

I didn't believe that for a second, but John's tone had grown gruff, and I sensed it was time to move on. "So am I going to have new, big muscles tomorrow and be able to lift couches with one hand?"

"That something you need often?"

I shrugged. "I was going to marry a big strong man to lift heavy things for me, but now that plan's scrapped, so I guess I'll be moving my own furniture for a while."

"For the record, I'll always help you move furniture," he said, his dark soft eyes meeting mine and generating a tornado of warm squishy happiness inside me. "But no, tomorrow you're probably going to be sore. You'll be strong later."

"So much for instant gratification," I pouted. "At least the shakes they have there are good." The caffeine was definitely taking hold, and I was feeling better about the world in general. Maybe it was being outside. Maybe it was the company. "What's next, Sammy?"

CHAPTER 11

JOHN

NO HOME IMPROVEMENT SHOWS
TODAY

We spent the next week following a routine. Wake up, fix a smoothie, listen to Joey grumble, and go to the gym. We took a rest day on Wednesday and finally gave in to her requests to stroll on the treadmill watching something called "Fixer Upper." I jogged beside her, music blasting in my own headphones, but I caught glimpses of her smiling and laughing along with whatever the people on her screen were saying. I liked seeing Joey happy.

Our workouts were slow—Joey was learning, and it was good for me to get back to basics. We went home afterwards, and I often headed to the rink while Joey told me not to worry about her and shooed me away. It was at those moments I wished Hank could talk. He clearly knew how my friend was spending long lonely hours at my house, but he didn't offer anything when I asked him.

A couple afternoons, Joey went with me to check out plans for the hockey camp that was happening in July.

"You organized all this?" she asked, her hands full of brochures and flyers as we left the foundation office and headed back to the car after I'd met with Elliott.

"Yeah," I said. "It started really small—just me teaching a couple of kids to skate. They approached me after a game, and there was something one of them said that made me want to help..."

"What was it?" Joey's hand clutched my arm, like if she didn't get the answer, she couldn't go on.

"This little guy, Alex. He looked up at me with these big dark eyes and told me that his dad had been a huge hockey fan and had always promised him he'd teach him to play... but..."

"Oh no."

"Yeah. I guess maybe I related?" I glanced into Joey's eyes and then looked away, moving again out toward the truck.

"You don't talk about your mom," she said quietly as we slid into the cab.

"No," I agreed. "But maybe this is kind of a way for me to pay tribute to her. By helping kids like me."

Joey didn't say anything, just watched me with those deep understanding eyes of hers as I put the truck in gear and headed home.

We'd spent the evenings on the couch, Joey forcing me to watch a show called "Suits" starting from the first season. Evidently it had a princess in it, but I was just happy to be close to a real-life princess on the couch. It was good to have someone else around. And it was incredible that person was Joey.

I kept Friday's workout short. We hit legs for a little while, and by the time we were headed out, Joey was whining, "tomorrow is an off day, right? Like a real off day. No treadmill, no nothing?"

"Yes. Rest day."

She was standing across from me looking through the open doors of my truck over the seat, which was at about chest level for her. "John?"

"Yeah?"

"I don't know if I can get up there. I'm sore everywhere."

A rest day was definitely needed. Maybe two. "Want a boost?"

She smiled at me and the way my insides turned to honey reminded me that I would do just about anything for this girl. I rounded the truck and wrapped my hands around her waist. "On three."

I counted and then lifted her up into the truck as she jumped, and when I moved back around to my side, my palms tingled from where I'd touched her.

Some of the guys from the team were getting together at Paddy's Friday night, and as we drove back home from the gym, I told Joey about it.

"It's just some of the team, a few of the wives and girl-friends. Just casual—totally social, nothing else."

She was looking at me across the center console with a strange expression I couldn't quite read, like she wasn't sure how to reply. "If I wasn't here, would you join them?"

"Yeah, probably." I didn't want to confess that I'd missed several nights out like this because I'd talked myself out of going. Sometimes I felt like a poor replacement for

Stephano Mizzoni, and it seemed like everyone else must feel that way too.

"Then we should go. Or, um—" Joey paused, her nose scrunching adorably. "Sorry, I just invited myself. That was rude. You should go. I can hang out with—"

"You're coming with me," I said, putting her out of her misery.

"Oh, okay. Good. That'll be fun."

"Yeah?"

"Sure. I'd love to meet the people you work with."

I let that sink in for a moment. The gorgeous woman at my side would certainly stir up some chatter among my teammates, and I had no doubt that a few of them might be interested in her, a thought that twisted my stomach. She might not be mine, but I didn't like the thought of any of the guys seeing her as a target of opportunity, either.

It was just after noon when we got back to the house, and each of us headed our separate ways to shower and clean up. When I found Joey again, she was on the couch, her phone in her hands and Hank seated just behind her. He was clearly seconds away from treating her to his tradi-tional head massage.

"Hank, no." I didn't think Joey would enjoy the hair stylings of the Burmese cat who'd adopted me.

Joey turned at the sound of my voice, and then spotted the cat. "How long have you been there?"

"Me or Hank?" I moved to sit beside her.

"The cat."

"He's stealthy. You know that's his favorite spot, though."

One hand went to the shiny waves that Joey had clearly just dried after her shower. I was certain she was contemplating cat claws tangled in the long strands just as I was. "Is he about to treat me to a massage?"

"He only does it if he likes you, so it'd be a compliment," I assured her. "Hank, get down." I gave the cat a little wave and he leapt down from the couch, shooting me a narrow-eyed gaze as he stalked away. "Sorry. Like I said, it's mostly his house."

Joey laughed and dropped her phone into her lap, letting her head fall back and then turning to look at me with those wide blue eyes. "It's so good to spend time with you, Sammy." Her voice was light, almost a whisper.

"It's really good to see you too."

"I'm so sorry it's been so long," she said.

"Hey, I could've reached out." Only I never would have. I'd known a bit about Joey's life after high school, heard from TJ about her engagement. She'd been on the path I'd always expected she'd find eventually, the one she was born for. Whatever we'd been was just a distraction from that preordained future.

She sighed. "I like seeing your life, getting to meet your cat."

I raised an eyebrow. "Yeah?" She didn't seem to be enamored with Hank.

Joey lifted her head and turned to face me, pulling one leg up onto the couch between us. "You need to tell me the truth, though," she said. "I know you weren't expecting me and I just totally crashed into the middle of your world here. If you need me to get going, just say the word."

So I could get back to beating myself up and spending every night watching myself fuck things up in replays?

"You showing up here was a fantastic surprise. I think maybe I needed a little distraction anyway."

"It's gonna get old, though," she pointed out. "You'll tell me when I'm wearing out my welcome?"

I tried to picture myself telling Joey goodbye, watching her drive away. The idea wasn't one I liked. I knew she wouldn't stay forever, but for now? I liked having her here.

"I'll tell you, but I imagine it'll be a couple years before I say anything like that."

"Years?" she laughed. "By then you'd be completely sick of me for sure! I've been on my best behavior, but I'm probably impossible to live with."

I shook my head, smiling at her. "I can't imagine that."

"Well, I promise it won't be years. I just need to get some things figured out is all." Her eyes clouded as she glanced at her phone again, and a wrinkle appeared between the dark blond brows.

"What are you figuring out?"

"Little things, you know. Like what the heck I'm going to do with my life. Where I'll live. My entire future. Stuff like that." She laughed, but I heard the edge of fear behind it. Joey was scared and I didn't blame her. Her life had gone from being dictated for her to being a completely blank slate.

"That's exciting, though," I suggested. "You get to decide. You get to do exactly what makes you happy."

She held my gaze for a long beat and then frowned again. "It sounds good. I guess I'm just realizing that I've barely chosen a single thing for myself. Not much that mattered, anyway. I don't really know how to start. Or what I even want."

"Your parents told you what you wanted?"

"Not in so many words, but yeah."

"Have you heard from them?" I gestured to the sparkly pink phone.

"Radio silence. Even Daddy and Granny T. Mama must've threatened them. They're waiting for me to break down and come back and apologize."

"That part of your plan?"

"Definitely not. But I don't know what my plan is." Her voice picked up a tiny whine, and I hated seeing her upset.

"In high school you were pretty determined to cure cancer."

"I was a kid."

"You got the degree."

"It's a piece of paper."

"That's not all it is, and you know it. I think you're scared."

"I'm flippin' terrified, Sammy."

She looked so sad and small in that moment, I reached out to drop a hand on her shoulder. It was instinct, a supporting gesture for a friend who clearly needed reassurance.

Joey looked up as I touched her, those crystal blue eyes meeting mine and holding them as something hot crawled inside me, spreading out and tensing. She shifted, moving closer, and my hand slid from her shoulder to cup the back of her neck as locks of her feather-soft hair slid across the skin of my arm.

How many nights in school had I lain there, dreaming of feeling Joey's silky hair on my skin?

I moved my thumb, marveling at the impossible softness of Joey's skin, and her mouth dropped open just a fraction, that full pink bottom lip catching my eye.

I realized what I was thinking, what my entire body was starting to believe, and was just about to pull back when Joey's eyes lowered to my mouth, and it was like she'd lit a fuse. The years of friendship and comfort between us spooled up tightly into a tense thread that had us just centimeters apart.

Joey's eyes found mine again, and I felt the tiniest nod of her head in my palm as my hand cupped it. Yes. She wanted it too. From there, logic and thought took a back seat to impulse and desire, and I closed the distance between us, pausing just before my lips found the perfect softness of Joey's mouth. I was waiting to wake up. Or for her to say no. Instead, in the pause, her hand found the side of my face, and tingles carried from her touch through the rest of my body.

This.

For years of my life, I'd dreamed of this.

And it had shown up on my doorstep without me even thinking about it.

Josephine Baxter was here. And I was finally going to kiss her.

Our lips brushed, and everything inside me sparked to life as if a switch had been flipped after years of being shut off. Electricity flowed to all those waiting cells throughout my body, lighting me up like a boardwalk carnival inside. I let my eyes drop shut as Joey's arms went around me, and colors shot across the insides of my eyelids, the sound of my own blood rushing through my ears.

The kiss was soft and careful at first, and then Joey moved, pushing herself against me and tightening her arms around my neck. I pulled her body closer, and felt her lips open beneath mine. I teased her bottom lip with my tongue, and the tiny sound that escaped her sent me spiraling. Our tongues touched, and soon, I was pushing her backward on the couch, laying my body out over hers, our mouths engaged in a give and take that felt like it could go on forever. Joey's hands pressed my shirt up as they slipped along the skin of my back, and all I could think was that I had finally gotten everything I'd ever wanted in the world.

We made out for what felt like hours, wrapped up in one another, arms and legs intertwined as our breathing turned heavy.

Finally, I began contemplating what would come next in a distant, lust-addled part of my consciousness. I could undress Joey—that was what I wanted to do. But once we went there, there would be no coming back from it. And the woman beneath me on the couch, my best friend, wasn't in a good place right now. I knew it, and so did she. And if a day ever came when I'd get to have Joey Baxter—really have a chance with her—I didn't want her to regret any part of it.

I just didn't think today was that day.

So, as hard as it was, I pulled back, bowing my head so

my forehead touched hers. I focused on her arms around me, her body as close as I'd dreamed it would be one thousand times before, and I forced myself to think of my friend instead of the beautiful woman she was. The friend who had left everything she'd ever known just days earlier. The one who was certainly searching, maybe even drowning.

I was going to work to help her find her center. But I was going to do that for her—not for me. If one day, when she was solid again, she turned back to me?

Then all bets were off.

But right now?

Right now, Joey needed a friend.

Her hands loosened their grip on my back, and we stayed like that, head to head, until our breaths slowed and the addictive frenzy surrounding us faded back into the afternoon glow of my living room.

Slowly, I sat up, my cheeks heating as I pushed myself to meet her gaze.

Joey's eyes were glassy, and she sat up slowly at my side, adjusting her top and pushing a hand absently through her hair. "Well," she said, her voice breathy.

"Well," I repeated.

"Handsome and a good kisser. Sammy, you must have the ladies lining up." Joey tossed these words out lightly, but something about them felt off, and I didn't like it.

"Hardly," I muttered, wishing I could rewind. I shouldn't have kissed her. Things were awkward now—could we come back from this? I swallowed hard, determined to be a good person. The friend she needed. "Listen, I'm sorry about that. I shouldn't have done that."

"No?" Was Joey flirting? The question was coy, but it was hard to tell. "Because really, I liked it. A lot."

She was going to make this difficult, I guessed. "I liked it too, trust me. But I don't think you need me kissing you right now."

Her eyes cleared and she fixed me in a laser stare. "I don't, huh?"

This conversation felt like it was going in the wrong direction. Was she angry?

"No, I don't think so."

"So, you're going to tell me what I need?"

"Well, no, that's not what I meant."

Joey stood. "But it's what you just did. My parents spent my whole life telling me what to do, what I needed. And now here we are, and you're doing the same damned thing." She never cursed. Saying "damned" was like the f-word for her.

She was definitely angry.

But then her shoulders fell and she appeared to deflate. "You're right, though."

"I am?"

"Yeah. I'm a mess. I'm sorry, Sammy. Maybe I just need a nap. What time are we leaving to meet your friends?"

"Uh, six?"

"I'll be ready." Joey turned and walked off to the guest room, closing the door behind her and leaving me alone to push down the very real feelings of attraction I was battling for my best friend.

CHAPTER 12
JOEY

CATS AND LISTS

I kissed John.

Or he kissed me.

As I sat on the end of the bed, replaying the event in my mind, it was all a blur, and if I'd been called upon to testify about what exactly had happened out there on the couch between us, I'd have admit I wasn't exactly sure.

He'd put his hand on my shoulder, and he did it in a way that felt like he knew exactly what I'd needed in that second, and given it to me on instinct. There was something so appealing about that all by itself. Because I wasn't sure of much right now, but I was sure I needed... something. Some reassurance, someone to tell me things would be okay. Maybe something more?

But the second his hand slid up to gently touch the skin of my neck, everything had shifted, and it was like the lid had sprung open to a box I'd pretended wasn't there all this time. The box where I'd put all the ideas I'd ever had as a girl about the hot hockey player and me.

And those ideas?

They'd been around since I'd challenged him to that very first race.

But I'd never been quite sure if John had them too. Sometimes it seemed clear that he did—I thought I saw it in the way he looked at me, felt it in that always charged air between us. But the one time I'd felt sure he might take the initiative back in high school... he didn't. And it had almost broken me. But John's friendship was too valuable to me to let it come between us, and so I'd accepted that we would always be friends, and that was all we'd ever be.

I'd spent the rest of high school telling myself he just didn't see me like that.

But this kiss?

This kiss said something different.

It had been sexy and hot, demanding and gratifying all at once. It had begun to fill some need inside me I didn't even know I had—like cool drops of water landing on the floor of a desert so parched it didn't even remember the last time it felt rain.

And then he'd stopped and told me what I needed. Or what I didn't need. And the desert had dried right back up.

I might not have been sure about a whole heck of a lot right then. My life was a battlefield with corpses of my past selves lining the path to where I stood now, staring at an empty horizon ahead.

I stared around the beautiful interior of my temporary room in my temporary home and contemplated everything that had happened in the last few minutes. And while uncertainty lingered within me, the attraction I felt for John Samuels was managing to overtake most of it in the form of questions I couldn't seem to stop from coming.

What happened now?

Why had John finally kissed me after all these years?

Was it something to do with pity? Or did he want me too?

And then, somewhere behind all those questions lay another. Was John right? Was I just reacting to my situation and unable to make good choices in the midst of all the uncertainty?

I flopped backward onto the bed and stared up at the ceiling, and a few seconds later, a green-eyed gaze set into a fuzzy grey-blue head leaned into my view, staring back at me.

Hank.

"Why are you in my room, Hank?" I whispered. There was no venom in my voice though. I was too confused to be angry now.

"Rrooowrrr."

"Right. I know."

One soft paw landed squarely in the center of my forehead and rested there.

"You trying to tell me something?"

Hank just rumbled his answer this time.

"Are you mad I kissed Sammy?"

No answer.

"I think he might have kissed me actually," I told the cat, who kept his paw on my forehead as if he was blessing me or giving me some kind of feline psychic reading.

"Hank?" I looked deep into the cat's mesmerizing green eyes. "I need to figure things out, don't I?"

Hank let out a very low "rrrrrr," the way my mama often said "hmmmm" when she was agreeing with something she knew I didn't want to hear.

"Should I make a list?" I asked the cat.

He didn't seem to have an opinion about that, but he lifted his paw from my head, as if giving me permission to get up. I did, moving to the little desk by the window, where there was a notepad and a pen in the drawer. (I might have done a tiny bit of snooping around that first night.)

I took the pad and sat in the chair at the desk, and for a second, I was taken back to being a little girl hanging out in my daddy's office. He had a little desk for me, and I'd sit and pretend to be a lawyer just like him. Only, I knew for sure I didn't want to be a lawyer.

I began writing words, trying to sort what was in my head into something that made some kind of sense.

1. Money
- Go home and apologize.
- Get a part-time job here.
- Put together a resume and start looking for a real job.
(Virginia?)
(Alabama?)

2. House
- Pay rent to John
- Get an apartment
- Go home and live rent free

3. Future
??

"It's a stupid list," I told Hank, dropping the pen. "There are so many things I could do, should do. But I don't really know what I want to do."

I did know one thing, though, and I crossed out the line "Go home and apologize," followed by "Go home and live rent free."

What was done was done, and I didn't regret that. I didn't regret stopping my wedding either.

But I missed my parents. Not so much their meddling and constant control of everything about my life, which, honestly, I'd hardly even noticed until recently. I missed them in a more general way. As people who I knew cared for me. Despite their misguided efforts to demonstrate it, I knew they really did have my best interest at heart.

The problem was that none of us knew where my best interests—or any of my interests, for that matter—really lay.

I thought about what John said.

In high school you were pretty determined to cure cancer.

I doubted I'd be able to do that, but I wondered if there

wasn't something to the notion. I had studied biomedical science. And I was still fascinated by the field. But while my peers had been getting real-world internships and jobs, I'd been spending long weekends during my last two years of college back at home, accompanying Evan to important dinners and events to help him establish his career. His life. Our future, he said.

And now that we didn't have a future, I didn't have much to show for that time. And I wasn't sure where to begin making up for it.

I sighed and dropped the pen.

Hank seemed to have lost interest in my list making, and had jumped up to the windowsill, where he stretched out long in the sun rays spread there to watch the street out front.

I followed his lead and stretched out on the bed beneath him, eventually curling into a ball and falling asleep.

When I woke, I felt better, if not any more clear about what I needed to do next. I pulled on my skinny jeans and a lacy summer blouse, touched up my hair and makeup, and carried my sandals out to the living room.

John looked up at me from the tablet he held. His face wore a look of uncertainty, and I knew I owed him an apology for snapping at him. It wasn't his fault I had no idea what I was doing with my life.

"I'm sorry," I began. "About earlier."

He put the tablet down and jumped to his feet. "Don't apologize," he said closing the distance between us. His expression was so open, so earnest. "Joey, I didn't mean anything by what I said. I want to help you, to make you see how many amazing possibilities you have in front of you. When I said that, I just meant, I didn't want to get in the way of you figuring things out."

I reached for his hand and squeezed, a little twist of nerves erupting in my stomach as I registered the roughness of his skin, it's warmth. "It's okay," I told him. "I know you want the best for me, and I also know you'd never do anything to hurt me."

"I wouldn't." His eyes held mine and that same fission erupted in the air between us that had always been there. This time, I did my best to ignore it, pulling my hand from his and stepping back.

"I'm just gonna get my shoes on and then I'll be ready to go meet the Wombats," I said, moving to sit on the couch and fasten my sandals. I was nervous to meet John's teammates.

"You say that," he said, his voice light and filled with fun. "But no one can really ever be prepared for these guys."

I looked up at him, hoping for more explanation, but he'd turned to the kitchen counter to collect his keys and wallet. I swallowed down my nerves and made myself a promise: Starting tonight, I wasn't hurt Joey leaving things behind. Instead, I was going to be strong Joey, building a future.

I stood and faced John again.

"Hey," he said, his gaze on my exposed upper arm. "I think I see some muscles forming there."

I looked down at my arm. It had only been a week—was I going to look like Arnold Schwarzenegger soon? I lifted my arm and bent it at the elbow like I'd seen men do when they wanted to show off their biceps.

John was right, there was a little change there, a bit of a contour I was pretty sure hadn't been there before. And oddly, I felt a surge of pride when I noticed it.

"Sexy," John murmured, and he walked past me toward the garage, leaving that word swirling around inside my head as I followed him to the car.

CHAPTER 13
JOHN

BOAT SHOES IN A BAR

Friday nights at Paddy's were a whole thing. It was a Wombats tradition to gather here when we were in town, and the rest of the town knew it and came out to hang with us. It was great being part of a small-town team. Most of the people who lived in Wilcox knew a few of us personally at this point, and none of them ever bothered us when we were out. They might buy a pint or ask for a signature on a coaster or a napkin, but it wasn't like the big city bars we went to as a team sometimes when we traveled, where there were selfies and crowds and insanity.

We were a fixture here, not a novelty.

One more reason I didn't want to lose my position on the team. I loved this town. I loved how much they loved our team.

"Nervous about your first full season?" A local guy asked after buying a drink for me and one for Joey when we stepped up to the bar. I didn't know him, so there was no polite way to introduce Joey, and the rest of the team had taken over the pool tables in the back, so we got waylaid on our journey to introduce her to them.

I glanced at Joey, who gave me a bright smile as she lifted her pint glass to her lips.

"A little, yeah."

"Big shoes to fill," the guy pointed out as if Mizzoni's shadow wasn't cast long and menacing over every one of my waking moments.

"Maybe you haven't seen this guy's feet," Joey said, grinning. She nudged me with her elbow, and while a rush of warmth flooded me at her confidence, I also felt like I didn't want to overpromise anything to this guy.

"I saw him at the end of last season," the guy said, turning to Joey now. He gave her a wink and then an appreciative up and down.

"Pretty impressive, right?"

I raised an eyebrow at Joey, who I didn't think had seen me play since high school, where ice hockey was certainly not as well-attended as, say, football. Alabama was not known for its winter sports, so those who attended really had to make an effort.

"All Star, maybe," the guy said, and my attention snapped back to him. Did he know that was my goal? Was he just messing around?

I couldn't help it. "Think so?" I asked him. As soon as the words were out, I wanted to kick myself. Why was I seeking validation from some random guy in a bar?

"Could happen," he said. "Especially with the support of a beautiful woman like this one." He wiggled his eyebrows at me.

"Oh, no. We're not—"

"He's got it nailed," Joey assured him, taking my arm in her own and steering us away from the bar. "Thanks for the drinks!"

I was about to ask her what that was all about, but she was already talking again.

"All Star, huh?"

"It's unlikely."

"If anyone can do it, you can. That's a pretty big deal?" She stopped us at a high-top table in view of the pool tables, where she must have seen the gathering of big and loud men who could only have been a hockey team.

I sighed and then looked her in the eyes. "Yes and no. If I could get All Star my first full season, it would help to cement my place on the team. It's not like it's a big deal, not really, not within the league, but it's a fan vote... and the Wombats management has a history of listening to the team's fans. If I got it, I might be able to relax a little."

"You're worried about your spot?"

"Yeah."

"But the other guy got hurt, right?"

I nodded. "And fell in love and moved away... His wedding is in September. In Italy."

Joey's eyes took on a distant look then, clouding slightly. I was about to ask her what was going through her head when Sly Remington appeared at our table, grinning from ear to ear. My protective instincts kicked up and I had to struggle to keep from tugging Joey to my side.

"Puppy dog, what do we have here?" He glanced between Joey and me and then stuck out a hand in her direction. "Apologies, I'm being rude. I'm just not used to seeing young John here in the company of beautiful women. I'm Sly."

"You're... sly?" she asked, wrinkling her nose and glancing at me.

"I am, but that's my name too. Short for Sylvester, but only two people in the world call me Sylvester. My mother and a tiny little hellion named Katie who I love just as much as I love her mother, my fiancée."

It was nice to hear a guy like Sly talk openly about being in love. It made me feel like one day, when I'd gotten the hockey thing nailed down, I might have a chance at it too.

"Sly," I said. "This is Joey. My best friend from school."

Sly looked between us, waggling his bushy eyebrows and breaking into a grin. "Friends, huh? I know a thing or two about high school pals."

"You do?" Joey asked him.

He nodded and turned to point at Clara, a dark-haired beauty with a brain to match, who appeared to be mopping the pool table with Corny and Freddy Elks. She high-fived Deck Gillespie, and then shot a grin at Sly and waved at me.

"She was my tutor. I was the dumb jock. When I came home last summer, she was back and she had a sidekick with her—her daughter, Katie."

"And now you're engaged?" Joey clasped her hands beneath her chin, wearing a wide smile.

"Yep. So let this be fair warning to you," he said, pointing between us. "Odds are good you'll end up married."

Joey swung her eyes to me, and I found our gazes locked, a hot, tense energy fizzing between us. I dragged my eyes away, my stomach twisting.

"Let me introduce you. I think Clara's just about done cleaning the floor with our teammates," Sly said, waving Joey over to the other side of the bar. I watched her go with him, recovering from the heated look we'd just shared.

I didn't want to want Joey. I'd been doing a good job keeping my ages-old desire for her tamped down, but the kiss earlier had knocked me off balance. And Sly's words didn't help.

I watched as Joey greeted Clara, her trademark smile and southern charm firmly in place as everything within me whimpered with the same boyish want I'd felt all through high school. She was perfect. But no amount of heated looks or stolen kisses would ever make her mine. Her family had made that very clear, and though she was an adult now, I knew they still had significant sway over her. I wasn't willing to wade into those waters again, believing it to be safe, while a monster catfish lurked just beneath the surface.

"You gonna stand here staring at the hot blonde all night?" Simpson and Corny made their way to my side. "Want us to give you some pointers?"

Corny sounded serious, but Cade gave him a whack on the shoulder. "Everyone knows you've got no game," he scoffed.

Corny's face lengthened as his brows went up and his mouth dropped open. "Me? You're the one with this whole

Viking aesthetic. I don't think that's quite the draw you think it is."

"At least I'm not wearing boat shoes in a bar."

We all looked down at Corny's feet. He was wearing Sperry Topsiders. I looked up and made a face. "He has a point."

"You want me to demonstrate my skills for you?" Corny asked us, angling his head at Joey. "If your shoes are getting in the way of closing the deal, you've got other problems," he said.

"That pretty little thing isn't even in your league," Simpson told him.

"Oh, and you think you could score—"

"I'm gonna stop you there," I said, breaking in before a discussion started that might end with me cracking someone's nose. "That is my best friend from high school. She's staying with me, and no one on this team better get near her." I looked between the guys, whose mouths had snapped shut simultaneously.

They stared at me, then looked at each other, and then looked back over at Joey. As if feeling their stares, she turned and lifted a hand toward me, beckoning me over with a smile.

"No shit," Corny said as I gave them a little salute and took my beer over to where Joey was talking with Clara and Sly.

"Sammy," Joey said, stepping sideways to make a spot for me at the little table by the wall where Sly had his arm around Clara. "Did you know Clara is a biologist?"

I nodded at the gorgeous woman at Sly's side. "I think I did hear that. Nice to see you again, Clara."

"You too," she said. She looked at Joey and then back at me. "I was just telling Joey that with her degree, she should really look into governmental public health, or even some of the private biotech companies springing up everywhere."

"Totally," I agreed. I loved that Joey had started a conversation about herself, about what she might want.

"I just have no clue where to start though," Joey said. "All my peers had jobs coming out of school. They'd spent their last years thinking about which path they would take. I spent mine doing... other things."

Clara tilted her head, but obviously decided against asking what other things Joey might have meant. "Well, if there's one thing I've learned at this point, it's that people might take different paths to get there, but success doesn't have only one door in."

"I'm living proof," Sly agreed, raising his glass. "Who would have thought I'd be heading into management?"

That got my attention. I'd heard that Sly was doing some office work for the organization, but I didn't realize how serious he was. "You finished an MBA, right?"

"Almost finished," Sly confirmed. "A few more credits."

"That's great," Joey said.

"So," Clara said, leaning across the table. "You want me to make a few calls? Maybe I could get you hooked up to do a shadow or two and learn more about a couple of the options."

"Seriously?" I could feel Joey's excitement vibrating out

of her at my side. "That would really be kind of you. I'd sure appreciate it if it isn't a lot of trouble."

"It's no trouble at all," Clara said. "And there's one woman I know really well at one of the veterinary biotechs that I think you'd hit it off with."

"Animals," Joey said thoughtfully.

Clara lifted a shoulder. "That's kind of where I operate."

"She wrestles bears for a living," Sly said.

Clara whacked him on the chest. "I do not. I track them and evaluate data about migration and habitat to help protect them."

"And wrestle them. When you're feeling spicy." Sly said.

"There is only one bear I wrestle, and he's on his way to solo hibernation at the moment." Clara's voice was sharp, but her eyes danced as she said this.

Sly pressed his lips together and shook his head, clearly not interested in losing his wrestling privileges.

"So you live here now? In Wilcox?" Clara asked Joey.

Joey glanced at me. "I mean, not really. I'm staying with John while I figure some things out. Just visiting I guess."

My heart dropped a bit at the thought of her leaving. I knew it was inevitable, but I hoped it wouldn't happen soon. Maybe it would be for the best, though. Joey was a good distraction, but she was exactly that. And I probably couldn't afford a distraction when I had so much on the line this season.

"Well, hopefully you'll be around long enough to get a taste of the kinds of things you could do for work—there are probably similar things back where you're from," Clara said. "And if you ended up going government, I know you'd find something. There's a real shortage in that field all over the country."

Joey nodded thoughtfully. "Thanks so much."

"Let me get your number. I'll call you next week," Clara promised, exchanging information with Joey.

"Get you another drink?" I asked her when Sly and Clara had wandered off to play another round of pool.

"Sure," Joey said, hopping up on to a stool and glancing around. She looked happy, lighter.

When I returned with our drinks, she was flanked by two guys I was pretty sure I'd already told to stay away from her. But Joey was laughing gleefully at something Simpson said, and Corny and his Topsiders seemed to be minding their manners.

"You and Joey have known each other for how long?" Simpson asked me as I handed Joey her beer.

"Uh, forever?" I laughed. "Fifth grade, Joey?"

"Sounds right. I had to save him when he almost died."

Corny and Simpson exchanged a wide-eyed look. "Do tell," Simpson said, leaning in.

I braced myself for the humiliating story of the mile run, but that's not what Joey told them. Instead, she told the story but made it about hydration and our evil elementary school teacher, and then went on to talk about my victorious mile the next year—for which I'd prepared and actually eaten and had water in my system.

"Hydration is important," Corny quipped.

"Especially in Alabama," Joey confirmed.

"That's where your charming accent is from," Simpson said.

Joey blushed and I fought the urge to trace the pink in her cheeks with my thumb.

"So if you two grew up together, why does Puppy here sound hillbilly while you're one-hundred percent southern belle?" Leave it to Corny to dig a little too deep.

"Cuz I'm from the wrong side of the tracks," I told them, not wanting Joey to have to spell it out. "Which is why her family was never too happy when I came around. Joey was always destined for greater things."

"Look how that turned out," she said, wrapping her arm through mine and leaning into my side, sending reassuring warmth through me, along with pings of something much less innocent. I loved the way she claimed me in front of my teammates, the way she touched me.

"It's gonna turn out fine," I told her, wanting to give her the same reassurance she'd just given me without even real- izing it. "You'll see."

Simpson and Corny headed back to the bar, and eventu- ally we all settled into a few tables with some wings and nachos. As the clock neared eleven, we agreed to call it a night. No one got rowdy or out of control—it might have been the off-season, but most of us were still focused on training. This was our time to recover and rehab, not to get so out of shape we didn't have a chance of coming back. Me especially.

As I helped Joey into the truck, she looked back at me. "I had fun with your team, John. I really like them."

"I'm glad," I told her, admiring the way the streetlight over the truck lit Joey's hair in shades of gold and pink.

"They think a lot of you," she said.

I wasn't sure how to respond, so I carefully shut her door and headed around to the driver's side. As I got in, she pressed on. "You don't think so."

"Think what?"

"You don't think your teammates admire you."

I tried to play that one off. She'd gotten awfully close to the real seed of my insecurity. "I'm still earning that," I told her.

"They know."

I started the truck, but paused, looking over at her. "Know what?" I couldn't resist asking.

"They know you're a superstar."

That was an exaggeration, but it felt good to hear. A warm glow of pride lit in my chest at the thought that she might see me that way.

We were quiet on the short ride home, and I tried not to wonder what might happen when we arrived. Would I have a chance to kiss Joey again? Would she want me to? Once we'd gotten back into the silent house, we found ourselves staring at one another as we stood in the kitchen.

"So," I said, wishing this awkward uncertainty hadn't followed us through the door. I turned and poured two glasses of water, just to give my hands something to do.

"So," Joey said, accepting hers and taking a step closer to where I stood, one hand on the counter.

"You had fun?"

She sipped her water and I dragged my eyes away from the slim column of her throat. God, she was sexy. "I did."

"I'm glad," I said, sipping my own water. When I put down the glass, Joey's eyes raked my face, lingering on my lips and sending blood coursing at high speed through my body.

"Sammy," she whispered, putting her glass down on the counter and stepping so close we were just inches apart. She stared up at me, her eyes unfocused and her chest heaving.

I couldn't take it. I should have turned and gone to bed, but I couldn't do it. The look in her eyes, the suggestive tilt of her head. There was no question what she was thinking about it, and dammit—I tried to be a good guy, but I had limits too.

I put down my water and dropped a hand to Joey's hip. She sucked in a sharp breath at the contact, her eyes never leaving my face.

My other hand rose of its own accord, and I watched my fingers trace a soft line down the side of Joey's cheek. Her eyes dropped shut for a second, and then opened again, finding my mouth. She leaned in closer, her chest meeting mine and forcing me to take a bracing breath to keep myself from lunging at her, devouring her.

When Joey's arm came up, reaching for me, wrapping around my neck, I was lost.

I dropped my head and our lips crashed together, and every bit of the tension I'd felt between us all night wrapped around us, pulling us together in a frenzied dance of hands, lips, bodies.

I knew this would change everything, but in that moment, I didn't care.

CHAPTER 14
JOEY

TALKING TO HANK

All I'd been able to think about since the kiss on the couch was the way it had felt to be the sole focus of John's attention. I'd known him forever, but my best friend had always been laser focused on success. First in school, then in hockey.

I'd never questioned why. John had good reasons to escape his circumstances and his athletic talent was his ticket.

But I'd never wished that focus might waver for a few moments as much as I wished for it now. Or really, as much as I'd started wishing for it as soon as I'd arrived in Virginia and seen him again.

John was everything he'd been in school—kind, conscientious, respectful. But now, in addition to being incredibly talented, he was also ridiculously attractive. Truth be told, I'd always been attracted to John, and there was a time when I'd been certain it was mutual—I'd even convinced myself he'd take me to his hockey banquet senior year.

But the way I felt about him in high school was nothing like the almost painful desire I had for him to put his hands on me now. I wanted him in a way that was foreign to me, startling. I'd had intimate moments with Evan, of course, but they'd never zinged with fire and tension like the few moments I'd spent in John's arms.

A distant part of me worried this was what a rebound felt like—I didn't know, since I'd never had enough experience to need to rebound. A date here and there, nothing too exciting until I'd started seeing Evan. And we knew how that turned out.

But this?

I didn't know if it was our shared history, or the somewhat random nature of our reunion, and I didn't really care. Because at that moment, John was kissing me, and it was everything.

Fire.

Ice.

Cataclysm.

Rebirth.

I pulled him closer to me, feeling like I needed to be part of him, melded with him, and he responded by scooping me off my feet with one arm banding my back and the other lifting me under my butt. My mind was a rushing swirl, and I lost track of everything but him. I expected we'd turn toward the bedrooms, but instead, John backed me up until I was sitting on his kitchen counter, my knees on either side of him and his mouth on mine.

My hands explored all the hard ridges and planes of muscle on his back, the soft threads of his thick dark hair.

And my mouth couldn't get enough of his clever tongue, his delicious lips. Soon I was writhing where I sat, pulling him close to relieve the building pressure at my core.

For a terrifying moment, John stepped back, pulling his mouth from mine and leaving me with a gaping emptiness where he'd been. Oh god, don't let him change his mind.

But the full lips I loved pulled into a lazy smile as John's dark eyes found mine, and his hands moved to my waist again, tracing lines up beneath the hem of my shirt.

"Take it off," I begged, needing his hands on my skin, needing contact and heat and...something.

He didn't waste time, lifting the shirt over my head and then making a noise in the back of his throat as he looked at me—half groan, half gasp.

"You're so beautiful, Joey. Every bit of you."

His words made me bold, and more than that—I believed them when he said them. Evan had said similar things, but in those situations, it had always felt like Evan's compliments were somehow about himself. As if my attributes only mattered because they reflected him.

But John? His face told me everything I needed to know. His warm eyes and easy smile had morphed into something close to adulation as he looked at me, and when his hands slid across my bare skin, it was like his touch was bonding us together, sealing our skin.

I pulled at the back of his shirt until he helped me and pulled it off over his head. His hands found my breasts, cupping me through the lacy fabric of my bra as his mouth left hot little trails across my chest. Just when I thought I would explode from the anticipation, he snapped open my bra and removed it, his thumb finding one hard nipple as he took the other in his mouth. I heard myself gasp as my hands ran through his hair, pulling him to me.

John took his time, licking and nipping my breasts, my stomach, rising again to take my mouth. And I pulsed and vibrated there on the counter, desperate both to have him and to never have this moment end. Our kiss had unlocked the door I'd thought I'd sealed shut—the one I'd wanted to open in high school, the one it had become clear John would never walk through.

But now?

We weren't in high school anymore. Things had changed. So many things. And as my best friend unsnapped my jeans and pulled them carefully down, helping me remove one leg and then the other, it was clear that the door had been blown wide open. And we were moving through.

John peeled my jeans from my legs, helping me out of my sandals as I watched him—careful, courteous.

And then, he lowered himself, his big hands landing on the outsides of my thighs as his hot breath hit my center, pulling a groan from somewhere deep inside me. God, I wanted... something. This. More. Everything.

When he brought his tongue to the fabric between my legs, swiping one hot, firm, confident lick up my center, I heard myself invoke the name of god. And when he slipped the fabric to the side and began systematically breaking through every last one of my rational thoughts using his tongue, his fingers... I let go.

"John, I can't... I don't..."

"Do you want me to stop?" he paused, ever the gentleman.

"No!" I nearly yelled it. "I just don't know if I can..."

"Yeah, you can," he whispered, his breath hot right where I needed it.

One of his arms went around the back of me, scooting my ass closer to his face at the edge of the counter. He left that arm there, bracing me as I raked both hands into his hair and tossed my head back, sensation rolling through me and cresting into a wave I thought might actually kill me when it broke.

"There you go, baby. Good girl." John's soft words sent me flying over the edge. Some girls needed dirty talk, I knew. But it turned out, all I needed was to hear John Samuels call me his baby, his good girl, and I was done for.

I was just coming down, returning to myself, when John rose and scooped me from the counter and into his arms. He held me against his chest like I weighed nothing, and moved his head to wipe his mouth across his shoulder before kissing me fiercely.

"That was..."

"Not done," John said, carrying me through the house and into his bedroom at the end of the hall. He deposited me gently in the center of the big wide bed, and then smiled down at me. "You need anything?"

"Only you," I told him, reaching for him.

The look that crossed his face at those words nearly sent me over the edge again, and I knew in that moment that this could become complicated. These feelings—mine and his—they weren't simple. They were bound up in years of mutual admiration, teenaged lust, and deep-rooted friendship. I didn't know what the outcome of tonight's time together would be, but I was lucid enough to know it would change something between us forever.

But it didn't matter. I couldn't stop it. I wanted it too much.

John stretched out over me, kissing me for long leisurely moments as if we had all the time in the world.

His palm slid up the side of my body, leaving a trail of heat in its wake.

"Your pants," I said, realizing he was still clothed.

He rolled and removed them, having pushed off his shoes in the kitchen, and then moved back to rest at my side. I let my own hand slide down the planes of his body and finally stop when I found what I sought. When my fingers wrapped him, his eyes dropped shut and he inhaled a long, shaky breath.

I stroked him, loving the way he moved in my hand. I tested different rhythms and pressures, measuring his reaction in the fervor with which he kissed me. Finally, he grunted and shifted his weight so he was on top of me, pushing my hand away, but never letting my mouth go for more than a second.

He leaned to the side, and I heard him rummaging in a drawer, then he was kneeling over me again, sliding a condom onto his length as my body coiled in preparation. My cells vibrated, my mind fizzed and popped, and everything inside me quivered with need.

John leaned forward again, kissing me gently as he notched himself at my entrance. My hands found his back, and I pressed and pulled, wanting him closer, faster. But he took his time, sliding into me a centimeter at a time and then back out, kissing me with each soft thrust until I couldn't take it anymore.

I lifted my hips, taking him in, and that seemed to trigger a spring inside him. He pumped with a grunt, and the sound of his feral need just about threw me off the top of that high cliff again. I wanted him, and there was no doubt he wanted me every bit as much—it was as stimulating as the act itself to know every ounce of desire was mutual.

John pulled out again and then thrust into me, and I encouraged him, lifting my hips, unable to stop the noises coming from deep inside me. He pumped and I took it, each thrust awakening something in me that was primed to explode.

When it happened, it was practically simultaneous, and I came with my eyes on John's handsome face. Watching the pleasure I saw there, knowing I'd given that to him was satisfying. And when his eyes found mine and he gritted his teeth together just before letting out a guttural stream of words, I felt like I'd won a prize. John fell back over me, bracing his weight with his forearms as his back heaved under my hands.

"Amazing," I said.

"Amazing," he repeated.

After a little while, he rolled to the side of me and excused himself to clean up. He came back with a warm washcloth and snuggled back in at my side, and I rolled to face him in the darkness. I could see his face in the glow from the clock at his bedside, and I traced the outline of his lips now.

"You're so gorgeous, Joey," he said. "But I feel like I need to tell you how much more than that you are to me."

"You don't need to say anything," I told him.

"I want to."

I put my finger in the center of his lips, stilling his words. "I don't think we should."

His eyebrows drew together in confusion.

"Let it be what it is. I don't want to ruin anything." I didn't want to examine what had happened because we might find out it had been a mistake. One we could never come back from. And just in case that was true, I didn't want him to make it worse. Some part of me thought he might regret what we'd just shared, and I didn't think I could take it if he said words he didn't mean on top of everything else. "I just want to enjoy the moment."

His dark eyes dropped shut and I thought he'd gone to sleep, but after a moment they opened again, something sad hiding in the depths. "Okay, Joey."

I drifted to sleep, everything inside me hoping maybe one day I'd hear him call me baby again.

When I woke, for a moment I wasn't sure quite where I was. But the big bed around me, and the soft blue sheets covering me all smelled like John, and the night before came rushing back. I stretched, reaching to my side and hoping to find him there, but all I found was empty sheets. I opened my eyes and stretched, sore in so many different ways, but all of them good. All of them reminding me that my life had shifted dramatically, and this pain was growth. My biceps and hamstrings reminded me that I'd increased my weight the last time I'd worked out—I was getting stronger. And my abs twinged when I moved. Soreness meant progress, meant change. There was something delicious about knowing I had done that—I was controlling it.

And then there was the soreness between my legs. I still wasn't sure what to make of the developments between John and me. Could we go on now as if nothing had happened? Did I want to?

I was about to rise, to follow the smell of bacon that I detected wafting from the front of the house, when Hank leapt onto the bed beside me. He stalked slowly up from the foot toward my head, his green-eyed gaze inscrutable as he took careful steps through the twisted sheets.

"I know what you're thinking," I told him, feeling awkward in front of the cat suddenly, like I'd done something wrong. "But Sammy and I have been friends forever."

The cat dropped his back end next to my shoulder and continued to inspect me with his assessing stare. He didn't say anything—and the fact I thought he might was probably of concern, but my head wasn't quite straight.

He was probably thinking that it was wrong of me to come in here, messing up John's life and now starting something between us that would probably go nowhere because I had no idea where I was going.

"I know," I moaned. "You're probably right." I sat up and

sighed, pulling the sheet up to cover myself in front of Hank.

Hank lifted a paw to inspect, licked it and rubbed it along the side of his face, and then dropped it again, his attention returning to me. He seemed to be suggesting that I couldn't avoid whatever discussion John had been trying to start last night forever.

"I should go talk to him. I know you're right."

"Are you talking to Hank?" John appeared in the doorway, dressed for the gym. He leaned one arm up high on the door, making his muscles pop as he tilted his head to look at me.

"Maybe." I hugged the sheets tighter to my body. I was clearly losing my mind. I had been talking to the cat. I'd actually been conversing with the cat, if you wanted to get technical.

"He's a good listener. Kind of judgmental, though," John said, a smile in his tone.

"He is," I agreed. "I'm worried he's judging me right now."

"He probably is," John dropped his arm and stepped into the room. "But his is only one opinion. And his experience of the world is fairly limited."

I looked at the cat, who seemed fairly confident in his opinions despite John's suggestion that he wasn't terribly worldly.

"Anyway, I made some bacon and eggs," he said. "Came in to see if you were ready to get up."

"No green smoothie today?"

"I made those too."

I made a face, though I was coming to like John's protein smoothies. "But bacon, you say?"

"Yes, Joey. There's bacon."

"Real bacon or that turkey stuff I saw in the fridge?" John seemed determined to substitute all the good things I loved with lesser versions that I did not love.

"I made both." John lowered himself to the foot of the bed, and then crawled over my legs until he reached my face. "We'll eat," he whispered, just inches from my mouth, his dark eyes glowing. "And then we can go work out."

I was about to protest, but his mouth found mine, and my brain began to short-circuit. Just as I relaxed into the kiss, it occurred to me that I hadn't even brushed my teeth. I pulled back and threw a hand over my mouth. "Dragon breath," I said.

"Not even close," John answered, his voice sexy and gruff. "But if you hadn't stopped that, the eggs would've gotten cold."

I raised an eyebrow. "I could eat cold eggs."

"Don't tempt me."

"Don't move," I told him, dashing out from beneath the covers to the guest room bath where my toothbrush lived. I returned to John's room a few minutes later, to find him on his back, arms crossed behind his head.

"You look awfully smug," I told him, lingering in the doorway. I'd pulled on the Wombats shirt he'd loaned me.

"Yeah?" he asked, a lazy smile taking over his face. "Wanna see if you can desmugify me?"

I moved toward the bed, crossing my arms as I stood at the foot. "That is not a word."

"Prove it," he said. But before I could do anything of the sort, he sat up quickly and reached for my hand, tugging me onto the mattress with him. I let myself be guided over him until I was lying on top of him, our faces just inches apart.

"Is this a good idea?" I asked, wanting to kiss him more than I could remember wanting anything.

"I think it's an incredible idea," he said, and his arms went around me as our mouths found each other again.

This morning's sex was playful and light, though there was plenty of the desperate need I'd felt the night before. But John let me work my way down his body this time, and just when I was about to take him into my mouth, he flipped me onto my back and took over.

We took turns exploring one another, and it felt like an equitable push and pull, give and take. And unlike any other sexual experience I'd had—it was fun. We laughed as much as anything else, and when I climaxed, sitting astride him with my head thrown back, it felt like everything was exactly right. The world was good, and happy, and I was here with my very best friend. A man I'd always loved at least a little bit.

"You're so goddamn sexy, baby," he said, pulling me down to kiss him again. And the word nestled inside me, cocooning into a soft nest where I could keep it safe and take it out whenever I wanted to feel loved and happy. John made me feel that way.

I realized, as I lay at his side, my hand toying with the ridges along his torso, that he always had.

"What are we doing at the gym today?" I asked him,

rolling to perch my chin on his chest so I could look up into his handsome face.

His hand stroked my back, sending warm shivers up and down the sensitive skin there. "Shoulders and core."

"Fun," I moaned, but my reluctance was mostly feigned. I liked the changes I was seeing in my body, the way I felt inside. I was getting stronger physically, and surprisingly, it was making me feel strong in other ways.

John kissed me again and then we slid out of bed and went to eat and work out.

It was a darn near perfect Sunday.

CHAPTER 15

JOHN

WE DON'T SKIP LEG DAY

I t was hard to keep myself away from Joey at the gym. At this point, she navigated the place like a vet, loading up her own bars and only asking for help when she needed a spot. But today? Today I wanted to pounce on her every time she walked by.

Some part of me had reverted back to the kid I'd been the first time I'd ever considered dating Joey. Kissing Joey. Doing more... and that kid was doing an endless celebration dance and sprinting around inside my head yelling "Holy Shit!"

I'd slept with several women. But I'd be lying if I didn't admit that at some point during each experience, I'd thought of Joey. So getting to actually sleep with Joey? Was a lot like achieving some long-held dream. I was exuberant.

There was a part of me that worried, though. Why hadn't she let me tell her how I felt about her? Was it because she saw the inevitable end even as we got started?

The idea gave me a chill I didn't enjoy. I didn't want her to leave.

Despite my concerns, I wasn't about to walk away. I was desperate enough for Joey that I realized I was willing to accept the consequences when it inevitably ended. She'd go on with her life, and I'd figure out a way to pick up the pieces. Until then? I wasn't going to dig too deep.

Joey was sexy and sweet, and so easy to be with.

She didn't seem to expect much, and I was beginning to find one of my favorite things was to surprise her with little gifts or her favorite coffee treat. Even the smallest things— like remembering to stir a half packet of Splenda into her tea at night made her ridiculously happy.

I was starting to think no one had ever really spoiled her before, which was hard to imagine given where and how Joey had grown up. It made me wonder about things with Evan, too, though I was hesitant to ask.

Joey didn't seem upset about the engagement breaking off, and she didn't seem to be obsessing about the cancelled wedding or her parents' silence. And if I was being honest, all of that worried me. It felt like we were on borrowed time, maybe. Or like we were stretched out on lawn chairs atop an active volcano, pretending to be oblivious to the imminent explosion as we went through blissful days and nights of workouts, quiet dinners, explosive sex. But when I raised the issue with her a week later, she brushed it off.

"There is no reason to live your life planning for the worst to happen," she told me as we rested between sets on the leg press. "All that does is make you miserable."

I took a slug of water and thought about her words, her

upbeat attitude. "Right," I agreed. "But you can still be optimistic and recognize that there are consequences to your actions."

She pulled a plate off the machine and shot me a narrow-eyed gaze as she racked it. As she moved the plate from the other side and settled into the seat, rolling her head to look at me again. "Are you getting tired of me? Is this your way of telling me I'm wearing out my welcome?" Her pretty face was suddenly uncertain, the bright eyes dimming and her mouth tightening.

"No. Honestly, I don't think I'd ever get tired of having you around."

She wiggled her eyebrows. "Because of the sex."

I couldn't stop the grin I felt spread across my lips. "I mean... yeah, that's a nice bonus," I admitted. "But I don't think I'd want you to leave even if that wasn't a part of this. I'm just worried... at some point, you'll have to make some decisions, right?"

Joey turned to face the leg press and straightened her legs, flipping the handles holding up the weight and shifting it to her legs. I watched, mesmerized as she lowered and pressed the weight up at an angle, the sled gliding smoothly up and down as the muscles in her thighs flexed.

Joey had always been sexy, but the version of my friend that was emerging after even a short time joining me at the gym was the hottest thing I'd ever seen. Her lean frame was beginning to take on contours and ridges of muscle that only made her more attractive. She was becoming strong, and I knew it was affecting her inside too.

She re-racked the sled and turned back to me, her cheeks flushed. "I am making decisions, John. And I wanted to talk to you about them, actually."

We switched places, and I put the plates back onto the sled, adding another on each side and then sliding into the seat. "Oh yeah?"

As I pressed, Joey talked.

"Clara called Monday after we saw her at the bar that night. She has two people for me to meet, and we set up shadows for the end of this week and the beginning of the next one."

"That's awesome. Where?"

"Well, that's what I wanted to talk to you about. They're both local. So if either one led to an actual job, it would be here."

My heart leapt at the thought of Joey staying. Would we be an actual couple? Would this short-term fling become something real?

"That would be amazing," I told her.

"She also found someone for me to talk to in Tennessee," she went on. "And I guess they're pretty desperate, because I called the guy and we scheduled a phone interview."

"How does that make them desperate? You've got a degree, you're qualified, right?"

"I did the interview and he sent me an offer." Joey delivered this news without emotion, and I couldn't tell if she was happy about the offer, about the validation of her qualifications.

"That's incredible." But it was in Tennessee. I hadn't missed that detail. I pressed the sled up one last time, a little more force fueling my last rep than usual, thanks to the thought of Joey leaving, and I flipped the handles to engage the safety and then looked at her. "It's incredible, right?"

She shrugged. "It's nice to be wanted, I guess."

"And it'd be closer to home. Is it a job you'd consider?"

Joey held my eyes for a moment and her bottom lip disappeared between her teeth. "It's in a lab. Working with a genetic biologist and focusing on inherited diseases in children. The pay is..."

I waited for her to say it was disappointing, ready to console her.

"It's pretty incredible. They must really be desperate."

The disappointment I felt threatened to color my words. "No. You're just that qualified, and you know it. Joey, that's great. Congratulations." I stood and tugged my friend up into a hug. Only, when our bodies touched, it didn't feel friendly at all. Joey had become a lot more than a friend to me, and I was having a hard time ignoring it—or the pain I knew I'd feel if she ended up moving back where she belonged.

The hug went on a bit longer than was strictly necessary, and when we disentangled, we were both flushed, and Joey let out a giggle that drew a couple curious looks from some of the muscle heads nearby. I forced myself to think about golf stats for a moment or two in order to keep the erection I was fighting from winning out.

"When do you have to give them an answer?" I asked, sitting back down to recover myself.

"I told him the truth—that I was looking at a couple

other things here and wouldn't know for at least a few weeks. He said that was fine, which is how I know they're totally frantic to hire someone."

"No." I pointed my water bottle at her after taking a drink. "If they were really desperate, they'd be doing whatever it took to get a warm body in that spot. If they're willing to wait, it's because they want you."

Joey held my gaze for a long beat, as if trying to see if the truth was there in my eyes somewhere. Her blue eyes widened slightly, almost as if she was surprised to see that I meant it, and maybe even accepted that truth herself.

"You're a fucking catch, and they know it," I added. When Joey smiled, I raised an eyebrow and couldn't stop myself from adding, "and so do I."

Wednesday morning, Joey appeared in the kitchen in a silky blouse and a pair of tan pants, looking groomed and professional—and painfully pretty.

"Are you ready?" I asked her. Today she was going to be shadowing a scientist in health and human services.

"I guess so," she said, and a tiny tremble in her voice gave away her nervousness.

"You'll be great," I told her, handing her the green smoothie I'd made for her, along with two pieces of real bacon. "And remember, this is basically you interviewing them."

She bit into a piece of bacon and her eyes dropped shut.

After she swallowed, she looked at me again. "And if it all goes wrong, I'll still have bacon."

"And me," I told her, wrapping an arm around her waist and dropping a kiss to her forehead. "But it won't. You'll do well, and they'll be drooling to get you in there full time."

"I'm just nervous," she said, sliding into a seat at the table. "I've never actually had a job, John. How sad is that?"

I slid her coffee across to her and took the seat across from her. "Not sad. Just the way your life has been so far."

"I have no idea what to expect," she said, leaning her head down and whispering like this was an admission of failure. "Clara told me a few things. She said this lady—Elodie—is really nice. So that's good."

"If you hate it, that will be an important data point," I reminded her. "You're just going to see if this is the kind of job you'd want. You're not committed to be there. If it's awful, you say no thank you and leave."

"I'm going to miss back and biceps."

I laughed. "I never thought I'd hear those words come out of your mouth."

Joey frowned at me. "I'm addicted," she said. "You created a monster."

"We could go when you get home. I need to get some ice time anyway."

Her face brightened. "Okay! That'll give me something to look forward to."

"Baby, you've got tons to look forward to. Your whole life is basically beginning right now."

Joey smiled at me and my heart twisted in my chest. I could see us, as if from above, sitting here across the kitchen table in the morning before work—a picture of happy domesticity. Joey and me... living a life together. Every day it went on, the more real it felt. It was becoming tough to remember that it was all temporary.

"I guess I'd better go," she said, finishing her smoothie and rising from the table.

"I made you a lunch," I said, moving to the refrigerator and pulling out a brown paper bag.

Joey froze and stared at me as I held it out to her. Her bright eyes shone, and her mouth dropped open. "You made me a lunch?"

"I mean, you don't have to take it..." I dropped the arm holding out the bag, deflated. I was ridiculous. What had I been thinking? But Joey hurled herself into my arms.

"Why are you so perfect?" she asked, pressing up to kiss me.

I kissed her back, joy flooding every cell inside me as my heart responded.

You're perfect. You've always been perfect for me.

CHAPTER 16
JOEY

E lodie Masters was tall and elegant, and very friendly. Within minutes of arriving, she'd met me in the lobby, handed me a badge with my name on it and walked me to the back where she pointed at a desk that would be mine for a few days. I dropped my things and slipped into the lab coat she gave me.

It felt so official. So grown up.

"I'm so glad you were open to this," she told me. "It's such a terrific way for us to see if we're a fit."

"I'm glad you offered. I'm really intrigued by the work you do here, Ms. Masters."

"Please," she laughed. "Call me Elodie."

Elodie showed me several of the studies the lab was working on, highlighting some of the interesting data they'd uncovered and explaining the various steps they would go through to report their findings and develop the technology once they had approvals.

At the end of the first day, we sat in her office, and I realized I should have been calling her Dr. Masters all along. "Do all the researchers here have PhDs?" I asked, feeling a little sheepish.

"No," she answered. "A few do, but lots of the techs are pretty recent graduates like yourself."

Dr. Masters explained a bit more about the various jobs and levels within the organization, and then she leaned back in her chair. "Tell me more about you, Josephine. What do you think you'd most like to learn about in a career field?"

For a second, I froze, searching my mind for the proper or correct answer. But then I forced myself to relax, John's voice echoing somewhere in my head, telling me I was strong, I was smart. And I began to talk, explaining to Dr. Masters the kind of work I'd envisioned ever since I was a little girl.

"That's pretty close to what we do here," she agreed. "I think you'd be an excellent fit."

I went back to John's that first day elated. Freedom felt amazing, and I couldn't wait for more.

Mama had started emailing me.

Dear Josephine:

I am getting in touch to suggest that you come home. Though your tantrum had sweeping repercussions, Daddy and I are ready to discuss things and help you attempt to reconcile with Evan and put things back together.

For now, I've told people that the stress of the wedding was too much for you, that you simply had to have a break.

If you like, we will send a car for you or arrange plane fare.

I'll expect a reply shortly,

Your Mother

They were all like that. They came every other day, and were formal and cold, and they made me want to scream and stomp and tear my hair out.

I wasn't a child—though I could be compelled to see that I'd handled my issues in a childish fashion instead of facing them head on. But head on had never worked with my mother.

And I didn't respond to her emails because they allowed no room for response. They were directive and hard.

I had no idea why she'd decided this was the best way to communicate—maybe because I hadn't managed to return her calls, and she'd never been fond of texting. But now she'd clearly set up some kind of rolling campaign to convince me that every choice I'd made since I'd dropped her off after my dress fitting had been an egregious mistake.

Only... it hadn't been. I wasn't ready to go home, not if going home meant ducking my head and stepping right back into that too-small box that had held my life before.

Now, for the first time, I felt free. I felt capable and powerful and strong.

It had been just under a month since I'd "run away from home." And while none of what I'd accomplished—including the wardrobe I'd had to buy to do the shadows Clara set up for me—had been done singlehandedly, it had all happened without the financial support or very tight strings of my family.

But it never would have happened without John.

I owed him some money since he'd been feeding, clothing, and housing me. But any time I brought it up, he refused to talk about it and wouldn't even hear of me promising to pay him back. Still, I would someday.

Our life together in his adorable house in Virginia had evolved into something so comfortable and domestic, I would never have believed it if someone had suggested this was what my life could ever be. There were no afternoon teas, no bridge club, no ladies' luncheons. It was a relief. And the real wonder if it was that despite the normalcy, the sheer regularity of it all... It was extraordinary.

It was like we were adults, playing house.

Except the way we played was different from how I'd played house as a kid. Less tea and cookies. More sex. There was a lot of sex.

I'd given up sleeping in the guest room, and Hank seemed to have given up judging me.

John and I lived together. We ate together, worked out

together, watched television together... and all the time in his presence reminded me why we'd been so close when we were young. We were so compatible. The thing neither of us knew back then was just how completely compatible we were—in every way. Especially physically.

All he had to do was look at me with those dark sexy eyes full of suggestion, and my panties were drenched. One of his full-lipped half smiles, and I'd be in his lap. The slightest graze of his fingers along my skin and my whole body lit up for him. It was addictive and electric, and unlike anything I'd ever felt before.

And then there was work, or the promise of it...

I shadowed Elodie Masters for three days, learning as much as I possibly could about the work she did developing novel treatments for livestock to help prevent devastating diseases that in the past had taken out entire herds. It was fascinating work, and Elodie was brilliant.

"There are lots of opportunities here, Josephine," she'd told me as we'd parted on my third day. "Give me a call if you're interested in talking some more about openings here. I am sure we have a place for you."

I'd been giddy when I'd gotten home each day, a sense of professional promise and possibility sweeping through me as John and I talked about what I'd seen and done while we worked out and had dinner.

The second shadow Clara had set up was actually in her own department, and it involved tracking emerging diseases in wildlife, seeking causes, finding interventions, and learning about possible threats of cross-over to the human population. At the end of that experience, Clara took me out for drinks.

"I don't know how to thank you for everything," I told her, sitting across from her at the little wine bar in downtown Wilcox.

She smiled at me as she lifted her pinot noir, raising it toward me. I touched her glass with my own. "Everyone just needs a chance to see what's possible," she said after taking a sip. "I think it's really smart that you didn't dive right into something straight out of school, actually. You gave yourself some time to really think about what you wanted."

I swallowed down my desire to explain that wasn't even close to what I'd been doing. It sounded so much better her way.

"Did either of those shadows feel like it could be a fit?"

"They both did," I said, soaking in the quiet cozy atmosphere of the little Italian-themed bar. We sat near the window, and the quaint Main Street of downtown Wilcox lay outside, making me feel like I'd gone back in time to one of those small towns in old Norman Rockwell paintings, or dropped into a Hallmark film. I loved it here. "Especially the first one. Dr. Masters and I really hit it off, and I really liked how much the actual science was a part of her everyday work."

Clara nodded. "It's exciting, isn't it? To take something you learned theoretically in school and see it applied to things that really make a difference?"

"Definitely." I ran a finger around the base of my wineglass.

"I sense some hesitation. What's the but?"

"The but," I repeated, laughing. "I have a but, but I don't know how valid it is really. A job is a job, right?"

Clara's head tilted and she frowned at me. "Not true. A job is something that will absorb about eighty percent of the time you're not at home, so whatever you're spending all those hours doing better be something you care about. Something you love, if possible."

"Yeah," I sighed.

"So what are you thinking? What's the real but?"

I told Clara about the offer in Tennessee, which was much closer to the world I thought I'd eventually go to work in—focused on human health and disease.

"Hmm," she said, her pretty face taking on a thoughtful look. "I could tell you that every advance and development we make in animal science has some kind of translation to human health, because it's mostly true. But I get it—if you feel like that's where you're supposed to be, I can't really argue with that."

I dropped my focus to my wine for a second, wishing the job that seemed like the best fit wasn't so far away. "Yeah, but I'm not sure I want to go back."

"Is Tennessee home?"

I met her eyes, realizing Clara was one of the few people I'd met in life who took me at face value, who didn't know my family or the preordained path I'd leapt off of.

"No, I'm from Alabama, actually."

"Oh," Clara said, her easy smile in place. She shifted her weight and moved her water glass as the waiter arrived with the flatbread we'd ordered to share. "And you moved up here to be with John?"

An awkward chuckle escaped me, and I tried to figure out how to tell my story in a way that didn't make me sound like a heartless and opportunistic bitch. But I only had the truth. "Kind of?"

Clara's eyes met mine and she gave a little head shake. "Kind of? Aren't you guys in a relationship? Living together? What's the kind of?"

I put my glass down and steeled myself to tell the story. "I was actually engaged down there. To a guy I wasn't in love with but who my parents adored. Our families practically arranged the whole thing."

The bright eyes across from me were intensely focused on me, but there was no judgment in them, only interest. I went on.

I told her about growing up under my parents' thumbs, about college not being quite the escape I'd thought it would be once Evan and I hooked up. I told her about dropping my mother off at home and pointing the car toward Virginia.

"So you were high school sweethearts?" she asked.

"Me and Sammy?" An unwanted flash of disappointment shot through me—the one unhappy memory I had of him from school. "No, it wasn't ever like that back then. I mean...I guess I thought it could have been, but that wasn't mutual."

"But you're together now, right?" She pulled a piece of flatbread from the platter and paused before taking a bite. "I guess I shouldn't assume, you just looked cozy the other night."

"We've kind of just fallen into something, I guess," I admitted. "I came here because he was the only person I could think to run to, the only person far enough away from Alabama who I knew would let me crash for a little while."

"So this is just temporary? Will you go back?"

I shook my head. "Not to Alabama, no."

"But maybe Tennessee is attractive because it's closer."

All of this had been in my head, but I'd actively avoided thinking too hard about any of it. Still, eventually my parents would need some kind of answers from me. I just wished I could find them for myself first.

"Maybe," I admitted. "I don't really know what I'm supposed to do. It isn't like my leaving was some kind of well thought out plan. I basically ran away."

"But you are a grown woman. It's in your rights to live your life the way you think is right."

I laughed. "You haven't met my mama."

We ate and drank for a while and the street outside grew darker, making the wine bar feel even cozier. Clara told me about Katie and her previous marriage to Katie's dad, and then she explained how she and Sly had gotten together after knowing each other in high school.

"That's so romantic," I told her, admiring the ring on her finger.

"So..." she drew the word out, and I knew she was going to ask about John.

"I don't know about that either," I said, beating her to the punch. I blew out a breath and then took a long drink of wine. "We're... I don't know. We're friends first. We've always been friends."

"When you get home tonight, will you go straight to bed? In a separate room?" She raised an eyebrow, a mischievous smile on her pink lips.

"I'm actually just supposed to text him when we're done here. He's picking me up. He didn't want me to worry about having to drive."

Clara was smiling at me in a way that made me blush.
"What?"
"You realize how cute that is, right?"
"He looks out for me. He always has."

The smile didn't fade and something about it made me squirm. "He's just a really good guy."

"Who you are sleeping with?" Even her words ignited thoughts of John's strong hands on my body and my blush grew hotter.

"Yes." It felt like an admission, but it was also a relief to have someone to talk to about it. "But it just kind of happened, and now we can't stop."

"Can't stop? Good, huh?"
"I can't even... it's like..."
"It's good."

"Yeah." I took a sip of wine, finishing the glass and setting it back on the table as I thought about what I wanted to say. "It's just like we've fallen into this rhythm. And it's not a bad thing, but it's almost like we went straight to domestic bliss and skipped all the whirlwind dating stuff. I mean, neither of us really ever asked the other about it, everything just evolved."

"It sounds really nice," Clara said.

"It is. So nice," I agreed. "But we also aren't really talking about the elephant in the room."

"The one wearing the big sign that says 'I just ended a long relationship, broke an engagement, and am essentially jobless and homeless'?"

"It sounds awful when you put it like that."

"It's not that bad. You're just in between things. You're deciding. And you have plenty of options."

"Yeah. But I need to make decisions pretty soon. My mother's been shooting across the bow."

Clara's eyebrows lowered and she let out a little laugh. "What does that mean?"

"Typical Mama stuff. Threats, mostly. Come home or I'll lose my inheritance. Come home or she'll never be able to show her face at the ladies' league luncheon again. Stuff like that."

"I don't know your mother," Clara began, her eyes dropping to the tabletop, "and it isn't my place to give advice. But I'll tell you one little thing and you can just tuck it away to think about later."

"Okay."

"My parents are both gone now, and when they were living, they spent plenty of time telling what I should and shouldn't be doing. And it used to drive me nuts. When I divorced Katie's dad, you would've thought the world was ending." Clara's lips turned into a sad smile, and she tilted her head. "But I can see now that it all came from a place of love. I was their only kid and they worried. It felt like meddling. But it was just concern. And love."

A sad little sigh escaped my lips without permission, and I sat lower in my chair. "Yeah. I know." I looked up at my friend. "I'm sorry about your parents."

"Thanks."

"I'll call her soon. I think I just want to be able to say, 'here's the plan' when I do. I don't want to leave any room for her to convince me that her ideas are the right ones."

"Easy enough. You already know what her ideas are."

I laughed, some of the heaviness lifting from within me. "True. I do. I just need to figure out what mine are."

"This was super fun," Clara said as we gathered our things and left after paying the bill. "Let's do it again if you stick around. And let me know what you decide. I'll help any way I can."

"I will. I owe you," I told her.

"Nah, that's what friends do," she said. I watched her walk to her car, which was parked at the curb outside, and I stood beneath the awning waiting for John. He took only a few minutes to arrive, but in that time, I considered every-thing Clara had said, and felt my resolve solidify.

CHAPTER 17
JOHN

OLD LIES ARE BAD LIES

I pulled up to the curb to pick up Joey with an almost uncomfortable happiness rising within me.

I'd had a little time to think these last few days while she went to work, and the conclusions I was coming up with were scary. At least they were for a guy who a couple weeks ago was unattached and uninvolved, focused one hundred percent on keeping his edge.

Suddenly, I was living a life of sheer bliss, coming home every day to a woman I loved, one I felt might have been actually put on the planet specifically for me. I'd always felt that way about Joey—it was only in the past weeks that I'd allowed myself to actually begin to acknowledge the possibility that it was true.

Fate and destiny were not things I'd really ever believed in. How could I? A kid whose life took his mother's couldn't let himself think about fate. If he did, he'd never survive the truth of his own existence. He had to think that things just happened.

But here she was. Josephine Baxter had arrived on my doorstep (okay, the police station) out of the blue and we'd fallen into a rhythm so natural it was hard to imagine it wasn't part of a much bigger plan. And where I'd been worried that this new life would interfere with my singular focus on proving my worth to the Wombats, it seemed to be doing the opposite.

Working with Joey at the gym had actually pushed me to work harder. I was stronger, leaner. And knowing she was waiting for me at home made my time on the ice more effective too. Corny and Elks had both commented on it last time we put together an informal scrimmage.

Joey looked up from her phone to see me arrive, and the smile that lit her beautiful face was everything. It was the sun and the moon. It was fucking elemental.

She pulled open the door and climbed in. "Hi Sammy."

"Hey baby. Did you have fun?"

Joey grinned at me, her eyes softening. "I like it when you call me baby."

I hadn't realized it had slipped out. God, I loved calling her baby. "You do?"

She nodded, the happy smile still lighting her face. "Especially when we're..."

I raised an eyebrow and glanced over at her as I pulled out, pointing the truck toward home. "When we're...?"

"You know."

Warmth mixed with the happiness in my chest and expanded, and I wished I could somehow freeze this moment. I wanted to take a three-dimensional picture of this exact second in time. I wished I could keep it and tuck it into my pocket to pull out and relive over and over, when I wanted to remember what it had felt like to be perfectly, totally happy.

"I do know."

Joey's giggle pulled my smile even wider.

"Think we should go home and I can call you baby some more?" I asked her.

"I think I'd like that," she said, her voice low and sexy and hot. She turned to face me, pulling one leg up into her seat as she swiveled. "But first, I want to talk."

If her tone hadn't been so light, so encouraging, I might have been worried. "Okay."

"I had such a nice time with Clara," she said, oblivious to the tiny flicker of fear she'd just launched into me. "She's super smart, and really insightful. And I can't believe how nice it was of her to set me up with those shadows."

"That was really nice."

Joey didn't say anything else as we pulled slowly into the tree-lined neighborhood where I lived, and I did my best to push down the seed of concern threatening to sprout inside me. We would talk when we went in, and whatever it was would be handled.

Inside, we settled on the couch, Hank in his spot behind me, preparing his paws for the head massage I'd get whether I wanted it or not.

"So," I began, wanting to eliminate whatever uncertainty lay between us.

"So," she said. "I think I'm ready to make some decisions."

"That's great." I said the words, but my stomach twisted.

Was Joey going to leave and move on with her life? Had this been just a pit stop on her way to her real future?

"It is great," she said. "And I want to thank you first, for everything."

Oh god. I braced myself for the goodbye.

"From the moment I arrived, you've been everything. You gave me a soft place to land, the time and space to think...clothes, food..." She flexed her arm, making her bicep pop. "And you gave me muscles!"

"You gave you muscles," I agreed.

"They're tiny, but they make me feel strong. It's like I got here, and you saw that I needed to get myself back, and you gave me a way to do it. I never knew that building my strength outside would result in making me strong inside."

"It does though, doesn't it?" I was glad to hear it. We'd really just gotten started, but I knew that connecting with your body could change your whole life. "I saw that when I worked at hockey camps in college. These kids who really had nothing would develop a sense of control over their lives... it's pretty incredible."

"It is," she said, her face glowing as she smiled at me. "And so are you. I feel so lucky that you were here. That you were so willing to help."

"Always." The word was almost a whisper. The suspense was killing me.

"Anyway," she went on, dropping her eyes as if gathering strength.

Hank's paws landed on my head, and I swatted them away as I tried to steel myself to have my heart broken.

Joey's mouth opened and at that second, the doorbell

rang. The melodic ring was followed by a series of loud, persistent knocks.

We exchanged a look as Hank leapt to the floor and wandered to the front door, ready to greet whoever was suddenly here.

"Um... hang on," I said, glancing at my watch. It was after eight, though it was Saturday. Still, I didn't have a lot of evening visitors. I didn't often have visitors at all. And the UPS guy wasn't normally so forceful about announcing his presence.

I stood, moving to answer the door, utterly unprepared for the two faces that greeted me on the other side.

"Hello John." Mr. And Mrs. Baxter stood on my doorstep, dressed as if they'd come straight from the polo game in linen and pastels.

"Mama?" Joey's voice was a mystified shriek, and she was by my side a second later. "Daddy?"

"Hello, Sweet Pea." Her father looked as comfortable on my doorstep as I imagined he did in his own home.

I struggled to find words, suddenly transported back to those times when I'd knocked on the huge imposing front door of the Baxter's enormous house in Peach Tree Grove. A scraggly kid from the wrong side of the tracks showing up to see the debutante who was way out of his league.

Finally, I managed a hello. Luckily, Joey wasn't short on words.

"What on earth are you doing here? How did you even find me?"

"Darling, it was no mystery where you were," Mrs.

Baxter said, glancing past us and into the house with a slightly annoyed look on her face.

"Your mother insisted on putting that app on your phone back in high school, darlin', remember? Plus, you told her you were staying with John, here." Mr. Baxter said, shaking his head as if he'd had no part in this decision to track their daughter via phone.

"John, dear, is there any chance I might visit your powder room?" Mrs. Baxter asked me. "We drove all the way from Richmond this afternoon."

"Richmond?" Joey said.

"Figured if we were coming to Virginia, we might as well visit your Aunt Louise," Mr. Baxter said. "We've been here about a week now." He grinned and I turned to see Joey's mouth drop open.

"A week?" she repeated.

"Come on in," I said, realizing we'd stand here in the entry for hours if I let Joey's clear shock run the show. "Mrs. Baxter, the restroom is just down the hall there, on the right."

"Thank you, John," she said, offering me a false smile before making her way down the hall. Hank let out a yowl when she passed, making her steps stutter briefly before she disappeared.

"Sorry to barge in on you, son," Mr. Baxter said, stepping inside and glancing around. "Though I guess maybe you're getting used to that now." He laughed at his own joke.

Joey stood wide-eyed by the door, still not quite recovered from the surprise of seeing her parents, I guessed.

"Can I get you a drink, sir?" I asked.

"Sure, that would be great," he said. "Got a good Scotch?"

"I've got some whiskey," I told him, hoping it wouldn't be inadequate held up to Mr. Baxter's undoubtedly high standards.

"That'll do, thanks." He turned to Joey, who still stood by the door, watching us as if she was on the other side of a screen. "Pumpkin, you want to come sit and tell me what you've been up to?"

"Um, okay," she said, glancing at me. I hoped she wouldn't tell them everything she'd been up to. Her look was almost guilty, though.

I poured four glasses of whiskey, unsure whether that was the appropriate thing to do in these specific circumstances. Did Joey's mother drink? Or would she be offended by the assumption? And would Joey drink in front of her parents? Did they know she drank? Was I supposed to drink?

Dammit, this was my house. And I was an adult. I splashed just a touch more into my own glass and took a quick swallow.

"Here you go, sir," I said, setting the glass on the coffee table in front of Mr. Baxter. "And for Mrs. Baxter," I said, setting hers down. I made one more trip, handed Joey her drink and then sat down across from Mr. Baxter just as Mrs. Baxter returned from the bathroom.

"Well, it's really nice to see you again," I told them, hoping the insincerity didn't come out too strongly in my tone. I wasn't much of a poker player since my emotions pretty much popped right out.

Mr. Baxter didn't answer, just lifted his glass to me and grinned before taking a sip. "Well, that's not half bad," he murmured, offering me a nod.

"No, thank you," Mrs. Baxter said primly, pushing her own glass away.

Joey reached across her father and took her mother's glass, setting it next to her own.

Mrs. Baxter let out a tiny huff.

"You tracked my phone?" Joey asked, her voice flat.

"I've been tracking you since you started driving, darling. I thought you knew that." Joey's mother waved a hand as if brushing this minor detail aside.

"We figured out you were in Wilcox since John plays here," Mr. Baxter told her. "But then we had to do a bit of detective work to figure out where exactly he lived." He leaned back, crossing his legs casually, as if this was just a meeting with his pals at the country club. "Your father sends his regards, John."

I felt my eyebrows fly up. "You spoke to my father?"

"Needed your address. The tracker isn't super accurate," Mr. Baxter said with a careless shrug.

I wondered what my father had made of that. Had he been on his good behavior, I wondered? Or had he been as offensive and rude as he'd been the one time he ate dinner at the Baxters' house when I was in high school? It was no shock he hadn't called to mention this little detail to me. My life was about as interesting to him as the local quilting bee.

"Darling," Mrs. Baxter said to Joey, sounding worn out and yet still managing to be condescending. "Why don't you gather your things and let's head home? I've managed to recoup half the deposit on the reception hall. We just need to rebook within the year. Replanning everything will be no small feat."

"Mama." Joey's voice was low but loud enough to hear clearly. "I am not coming home. And I'm not marrying Evan."

Mrs. Baxter straightened as if she'd been slapped. I doubted Joey told her mother no many times before.

The older woman sighed. "Haven't you had enough of this?" With the word "this" she waved around my house, and as I followed the wave of her smooth, manicured hand, it was as if my house was suddenly drained of all color, all personality, all class. I saw it as a woman like Mrs. Baxter might—small, spare, and sad.

"No, Mama. I'm not tired of it at all. John has been nice enough to take me in and help me look into some of my options."

"Your options, Sweet Pea?" Mr. Baxter asked, swirling the whiskey in his glass appreciatively. "This stuff is growin' on me, John."

"I'm glad, sir." I felt like a third wheel in this conversation, but I was trapped in my spot across from this intimidating couple. And I didn't want to abandon Joey, who had just gulped down her first glass of whiskey and was now sipping at the second.

Joey didn't seem in a rush to tell her parents about the "options" she'd mentioned, and my discomfort had my mouth suddenly attempting to fill the silence.

"This is a mid-Atlantic whiskey," I said, lifting my own glass. Mr. Baxter reached his out across the table and we clinked them together. The gesture felt slightly out of sync with the other conversation that was going on around this table, and I had an odd sensation of fracture—as if two separate times were occurring simultaneously in one space.

"It's called Half Cat," I went on, realizing there was no real purpose to my jabbering but unwilling to release the space back to the uncomfortable hesitation I felt from Joey. "They make it in Maryland," I continued. "And now I hear it's the signature whiskey of the Kasper Ridge Resort out in Colorado."

"Oh yeah?" Mr. Baxter said, his tone impressed. "I read about that place recently, I think."

"Can we get back to the point of being here, please?" Mrs. Baxter said.

Joey put her glass down with a thud, and I realized she'd just pounded both glasses in rapid succession.

Oh hell.

"The point of me being here was to get away from you," Joey said, her tone tired. "I have no clue why you're here."

Joey's mother's mouth dropped open and then snapped shut as a rosy blush climbed her cheeks.

"Pumpkin, don't speak to your mama that way," Mr. Baxter said, but there was no venom in his words.

Joey's shoulders slumped. "I'm sorry, Mama, Daddy," Joey said. "I shouldn't have just run, but you have to understand how trapped I felt."

"I do not," Mrs. Baxter huffed.

"Everything about my life was planned for me," Joey went on, her words slurring just the tiniest bit. "You chose my clothes, my fiancé, my wedding date..."

"Darlin', your mother and I just want to take care of you," Mr. Baxter said, raising his own empty glass in my direction.

I stood and retrieved the bottle, handing it to him. He grinned at the little cat on the label and poured himself more.

"I'm an adult," Joey said. "And I need to be allowed to make decisions for myself."

"Decisions like running away to Virginia to play house with the same boy who tried to ruin your future for you back in high school?"

That got my attention. "Sorry, what?"

Mrs. Baxter waved a hand at me, as if dismissing me. "You nearly made Josephine miss the most important social engagement of her junior year," she explained. "With that little sports dinner you tried to drag her to. And if she'd missed it, she might not have had the opportunity to make a good impression on the executive director of the ladies' league, who went on to write her a glowing letter of recommendation for college. And who was, incidentally, the mother of her future fiancé." Mrs. Baxter sniffed as she finished this little speech, and anger swelled inside me.

I remembered that dinner.

It was the one I'd asked Joey to after working up the nerve for weeks. It was the dinner where I was going to be awarded MVP, the one that marked a clear step toward the future I was pursuing. And it was the only time I'd been brave enough to act on my all-consuming crush on my best friend.

Joey had said yes.

But two days before the banquet, Mr. Baxter had called me, explaining that Joey was worried about our friendship and how coming with me to the banquet might give me the wrong idea. He'd made it explicitly clear that Joey did not think of me as anything but a friend. He told me she'd been too embarrassed to make the call herself. And I'd been too embarrassed to ever bring it up with her again.

"You told me John stopped by and cancelled that when I was out," Joey said slowly. I watched her face as the pieces clicked together in her head. I didn't know what else her parents had told her, but whatever it was had kept her from ever mentioning the dinner to me again. "You told me he'd asked you to tell me and that I shouldn't ever bring it up so I didn't embarrass him."

Anger formed a hard knot inside me.

She turned to me. "They told me you'd realized you couldn't afford to take me after all," she said, her eyes shining and sad.

Now humiliation joined the anger and my heart burned in my chest for the boy I'd been back then. That kid had saved and scrimped to buy a corsage and pay for the second plate at that banquet. That kid had put every hope he had on that evening finally moving his desperate crush into something real, something mutual. He'd been gleefully anticipating the surprise from his teammates when they saw his beautiful date. And when he'd gotten the balls to ask her, she had said yes.

But her parents had decided for her.

"That's not what happened," I said quietly, meeting Joey's eyes and feeling that years-old secret solidify the bond between us. Her eyes shone with sympathy and something much deeper, and she reached out a hand, grasping mine.

Then she let go and turned back to her parents.

"There is no point talking about the horrible things you did when I was young," she said, earning a huff from her mother and a quiet "darlin'" from her dad. "Because my life has moved on, and all the decisions I'm making from now on are my own, and I don't care what you think about them."

"Darlin', why don't you just come on home, and we'll talk about everything? We can let John here get back to his own life."

I waited for her to agree, to give in, every fiber of my being hoping she wouldn't, that the quiet touch of her hand had confirmed what I felt inside.

"Your house isn't my home any longer," Joey said to the astonished couple on my couch, her voice rising in pitch. "This is my home."

Mrs. Baxter glanced around, her face turning down into a disbelieving frown. "What on earth do you—"

"John and I are engaged. We're getting married."

Time stopped, and all three of us turned to stare at Josephine Baxter.

CHAPTER 18

JOEY

SPORTS PEOPLE. HM.

I'd had to say something. Something that would definitively confirm for my mother that I was never, ever going to be back under her thumb. In that house. Living according to someone else's wishes and rules.

The words had come out of my mouth without any forethought, fully formed and existing in the world before I could consider what the consequences of uttering them might be.

In the very short term, the consequences were complete and total silence, accompanied by wide-eyed looks, and from my mother, a tiny gasp. As the quiet seconds ticked on, I dragged my eyes to John, unsure quite what I hoped to see in his face but bracing myself for disapproval.

His dark brown eyes were big, fixed on my face with shock. And when I met his gaze, they blinked once, twice, and then I saw a little flicker of warmth light inside them. There it was—the silent reassurance he'd always offered me

—even when I'd just uttered the most insane thing he'd ever heard me say.

Before I could think about how to take the words back or fix the brand new disaster I'd just created, Mama was speaking again.

"Well, that is simply unacceptable," she said. "Besides the fact that the two of you getting married on the basis of some childhood friendship is ludicrous, let's take a moment and think about what people will say."

"Adelaide," my father murmured, but Mama ignored him.

"No, Franklin. This is insane. These two... children... are from completely different worlds. Well, they might as well be from different galaxies! He's a sports person, for god's sake. A Baxter—our one and only daughter, I might add— was not raised to marry a sports person."

Well that was ridiculous. I pushed down the fury roiling within me at Mama's clear attempt to mask her disdain for John's origins by pointing to his occupation instead. "He's a hockey player, Mama. In the FHL. The youngest starting goalie in the league," I told her, my voice finally steady. Though the detritus of the bomb was still scattering, I was comforted by the awareness that John didn't seem angry. And emboldened by two shots of whiskey. "He's incredibly talented."

"That is beside the point," Mama huffed. "I think you're not really getting married," she said, landing a bit too close to the truth for my liking. "I think you're just saying that to shock me."

I shook my head. "Why would it shock you for me to

choose my own life partner? To make any choices for myself, actually? Shouldn't that be what you want for your child?" The words flew from my mouth, dislodged by the whiskey, no doubt. I thought it was probably the first time I'd spoken my whole mind to my mother.

"Darlin', let's all just calm down for a minute here," Daddy suggested.

"No, I don't think we should," I told him, swinging my angry gaze his way. "Did you hear what she just said? As if John is somehow less than we are, as if being raised on the wrong side of Peach Tree Grove or going to a different college or choosing to use his talent to build a career makes him in any way less qualified for anything."

"Joey, it's okay," John said, his warm hand dropping on my arm.

"It's not," I whispered. "It's never been okay."

Suddenly, I just wanted my parents to leave and take their snobbery with them. I wanted them to have never shown up here and interrupted the new life I was in the midst of building. Their arrival had ruined everything—had forced something that on its own was so wonderful, so natural.

"I think you should go," I told them.

"You're not even wearing a ring," Mama said. Her voice held an edge of challenge, and I didn't have it in me to fight any more. I was about to admit that I'd blurted the words, that I'd made it up to shock them, when John spoke.

"It was my mother's ring, and it didn't fit quite right. It's at the jeweler's to be resized."

A warm reassurance settled the anxious nerves that had

been pinging around within me. John mentioning his mother was like getting a sighting of the Loch Ness Monster. The fact he'd said these words made me want to lean into him, curl into his embrace and just breathe him for a while. But my parents were still here, still shocked, still upset.

"Well," Mama said. As she sat looking lost and confused, I watched Hank leap to the top of the couch and settle directly behind her. He lifted a paw and licked it, then rubbed it over his face. I knew that routine. Mama was about to get a head massage, and despite everything, I was eager to see it.

"Yes, well." Daddy stood, extending a hand for my mother, and waving the cat away. I sighed. It was probably for the best. "Joey darlin', why don't we reconvene in the morning? Could we take you kids out to breakfast to congratulate you? Talk about what's next?"

I stared at him. Breakfast would just be another battleground where my mother could try the next tactic she'd developed to get me to give up and come back home.

John glanced at me, and whatever he saw in my face must've confirmed that I was not in a decision-making state of mind. "That would be nice, sir. There's a diner over in Boomsmack that makes great waffles and does a really nice Benedict," he said.

"We'll go there, then," Daddy confirmed, helping Mama to her feet. "Thanks for the whiskey."

"Any time, sir."

Mama didn't say another word, just walked to the front

door and waited for my father to open it, then disappeared out into the night, Daddy just behind.

John let the door close quietly and then turned to face me, and I couldn't read the expression on his face. He had every right to be upset with me for dragging him deeper into my mess. But he didn't look upset. He looked... happy?

"I'm sorry," I whispered. "I don't know why I said that."

He shook his head slowly back and forth and stepped close. I leaned into his strong chest out of habit and a need for reassurance, feeling lighter as his arms closed around me.

"I'd be the luckiest guy in the world to be marrying you," he whispered.

I turned my head to look up into his beautiful face, the one that had been part of my life since I was a little girl. So familiar, so comforting. And now? So sexy. "You really feel that way?"

He blew out a long breath, his eyes finding something in the distance to look at, like he was gathering strength from that far away spot. Then he looked back down at me with so much love and warmth that my heart actually expanded to be on the receiving end of it. "I think I've been in love with you as long as I've known you, Joey. Marrying you isn't a shocking idea to me. It's more like a fantasy I've had since the first time you beat me in a race."

His words were the sweetest I'd ever heard, and I tucked them down deep to consider later with the depth they deserved. For now, I smiled up at him. "Oh yeah? You've always wanted to marry someone who could kick your butt?"

He laughed, and touched his forehead to mine. "Something like that, I guess."

I slid my arms around his waist, amazed that we could create such a happy little bubble here in the aftermath of my parents showing up and trying to explode everything. Only John could make me feel like everything could still be wonderful and perfect.

"I think I've been in love with you a long time too," I told him, feeling the words forming like a truth just hanging there in the air, waiting for me to acknowledge it.

John pulled his head back and smiled at me, and then his eyes grew darker, and I followed his cues, tilting my chin up for the kiss I needed him to give me.

It was soft at first, maybe in recognition of our shared past, our mutual trauma, and the insanity we'd just survived together. But it grew deeper and hotter as it went on, and John's hands were on my skin, pulling my shirt from my body as I did the same for him. We made our way down the hall to his bed, and fell onto it together.

I reveled in the attention and intimacy as John removed the rest of my clothing, then stood at the foot of the bed smiling down at me. There was something in his smile I didn't recognize.

"What?" I whispered, pressing myself up onto my elbows.

"You were going to go to that banquet with me. You wanted to go." His voice was low and full of wonder, as if he'd just realized this.

"Yes."

His smile grew wider. "You said yes when I asked and you wanted to go. It was going to be a date."

"My parents lied to you, Sammy." I reached for him, and he took my hand, climbing to lie next to me. "And it broke my heart. I didn't believe their story, but I did believe you changed your mind."

"I haven't changed my mind in over a decade where you're concerned," he said.

As I helped him out of his pants and reveled in the feeling of him at my side, in my arms, filling my senses, a distant part of my mind considered the reality I'd been forced to face tonight. My parents had kept us apart with intention. They'd casually hurt us both in pursuit of their misguided attempts to steer my life in the direction they believed it should go. And it was a miracle we were here now. Together.

John's warm hands preceded his soft lips over my breasts, my stomach, my thighs. I arched and writhed beneath his attention, certain my body had never been this alive. Everything he did, every part of him, felt custom fit to me, to my body, to my hands.

We made love, feeling the universe contract around us. The entirety of everything narrowed down to a pinpoint for those hours, putting us right at its center, and there simply was nothing else. There was passion and pleasure, every cell in my body coming to life for him. There was just John.

And as the atmosphere thinned once more, spinning back out to include everything and everyone else as we lay twisted together in his bed, I rested my head on his chest and celebrated every heartbeat, matching it to my own. We aligned perfectly. We always had.

"So," I said, loving the feel of his radiant warmth and strong body beneath my hands, my head.

"So," he repeated.

"What the heck are we going to tell my parents in the morning?"

A low chuckle escaped him, and I felt it rumble in his chest. "I have no idea. You tell me."

I gave my mind a few minutes to spin, to circle all the potential paths until it landed on the one I kept coming back to, over and over. I pulled the blanket back up over us as I moved to John's side, pressing myself up to rest my head on my hand, my elbow on the bed. John rolled to mirror my posture and we faced one another. A soft thud at the end of the bed signaled Hank's decision to join in this conversation, and a second later, he dropped himself between our chests with a murmured "rrrowr."

"I basically manipulated you into an engagement," I said.

"I'm not upset about that. But Joey, even if it was a real engagement, I'd be worried. You just ended another engagement. This would be a rebound." A wrinkle appeared between John's brows and I saw the doubt cloud his eyes.

"That's definitely not true."

He squinted at me for a second. "Do I need to define rebound for you?"

"I know the definition. And I think if we really look at it technically, Evan was the rebound." My hand lay between us, and John took it now with his, turning it over and tracing light lines on my palm.

"How was he the rebound? You would have had to be involved with someone before that." His brows lowered as he said, "Oh, you were. The first part of college?"

He wasn't getting it, but there was no rush. We had all night. And maybe longer. "Before that," I told him.

"You were with someone in high school?" He pressed his lips together as he thought.

"Not the way I wanted to be, but yeah."

One eyebrow rose and the smile returned to his lips. "Is that so?"

"Maybe I didn't have words for it back then, or the guts to tell you, but I've been in love with you for years," I told him, my heart swelling with the glorious truth of it.

"I'm sure I don't have to tell you that was mutual," he murmured, dropping my gaze for a second like he was embarrassed.

"Was?"

The dark eyes found mine again.

"Is." A little laugh rumbled out of him. "Joey, baby, I have a feeling I'll be in love with you for the rest of my life, no matter what happens with your parents tomorrow."

"What do you want to happen tomorrow?" My heart was rising inside me. Was I really brave enough to suggest what it was hoping for?

"It's not my call. My cards are on the table. I might be an idiot, but I think we both know I'd do just about anything for you."

I swallowed hard, wondering if I was really going to be

able to give voice to the thing I was thinking, the thing I was hoping for.

"Would you marry me?" I asked, unable to hold his gaze while I threw out the one thing I knew I really wanted. "Not tomorrow, I mean," I added quickly. "But maybe someday?"

John held my gaze for a long moment as the smile on his lips grew into a full-blown grin. And then he rolled from the bed. "Stay there," he said.

"Where are you going?" I sat up.

"Just follow directions for once in your life, Joey. Stay there." John moved to his dresser and began digging in a drawer. He slammed it shut, dug in another drawer.

"This is a weird time to go hunting for your favorite jammies."

"Quiet, woman, you're killing the moment."

"Hmph." I channeled my mother for that one.

Finally, John found the right drawer and extracted something from the very back of it. He held up a tiny satin bag tied with a little string, and moved to the side of the bed with it. I turned to face him, my chest tightening as he dropped to one knee, opening the little bag as he did so.

"Sammy..." I breathed, the world condensing around us again.

"Joey," he said, but then a frown crossed his face and a sudden worry leapt into me. He shook his head. "Josephine Baxter," he began again, and my chest loosened. "I have loved you since you saved my life with a bottle of water in the hot Alabama sun on the playground. I've loved you every day since then. In little ways and big ones, when you were close, and when you were planning to marry someone else. I'm pretty sure I have never had a choice about being in love with you, so it would be a big relief and the ultimate honor if you'd agree to be my wife and put me out of my misery."

Sunshine filled every nook and cranny of my body as I smiled back at John, kneeling there naked on the floor of his bedroom. "You're proposing for real?" I asked, just wanting to make sure.

"I'm on my knee here, Joey," he pointed out. "I have a ring."

"It's a naked proposal," I giggled, so much emotion racing through me I couldn't quite sort through what things I should feel or say first.

"You want me to get dressed?"

"No. I want to remember this moment exactly like it is." I scooted to the edge of the bed.

"This is the ring I mentioned earlier."

He held the beautiful ring out to me now. It was gorgeous—a small solitaire diamond surrounded by a border of smaller stones, set in a silver band. "This was your mom's?"

He nodded, reaching for my hand as emotion clogged my throat. "What do you say?" he asked softly. "Marry me for real?"

Tears flooded unexpectedly into my eyes as I nodded and heard myself say, "Of course!" I reached out my hand and he slid the ring on. Despite the story he'd told my parents, it fit me perfectly. And I didn't say it to him, but this ring looked so much more natural on my hand than the enormous thing Evan had given me. Everything about John fit me so much better.

John's eyes were full of tears too, and as he reached for me, I threw myself into his arms. We knelt facing one another on his bedroom carpet, in a hug that felt like forever and held a promise of even longer. As I let myself cry—happy tears this time—Hank's paws found the back of my head.

"This cat," I laughed into John's shoulder.

"Hank," he hissed. "Beat it. Not now."

"Rowwr."

John lifted me to my feet, and we stood beside his bed in an embrace as the world around us went on oblivious to the joy radiating between us. Why had I stayed away so long? Some part of me had always known I belonged with John.

"I'm so happy," I told him, pulling back to see his face.

"You're sure?" he asked. "It's not too sudden?"

"I think I kinda forced the issue, but no. It feels right. Perfect."

"It does."

John spun me back into the bed, and we celebrated together—our first time as an engaged couple.

CHAPTER 19

JOHN

SAY THE BAD WORDS

When I opened my eyes, it took a few seconds for reality to sink in. My mind flicked through the night before like it was comprised of still-action shots. Adelaide and Franklin showing up. Adelaide's disapproving face. Joey's announcement. And finally, the two of us, alone together in my bed for hours. Joey wearing my mother's ring.

Her hand was splayed on my chest now as she slept on, the ring glinting in the gauzy morning light. Seeing it there created such a well of emotion inside me, I was having trouble sorting it all.

I'd never gotten to see the ring on my mother's hand, but TJ had, and of course Dad had. What would they think of it on Joey's slim finger?

The ring was supposed to be TJ's. Dad had given it to him when he'd begun dating Tabitha. But TJ felt like it wasn't the right thing for her—for him, the ring held sadness. He wanted something new for his fiancée. So he passed it on to me.

"What will Dad say?" I had asked him at the time.

"The question is what would Mom say," TJ told me. "And I know she'd approve."

It wasn't as if TJ had gotten a whole lot more time with Mom than I had. He'd been only three when she died just after I was delivered. But he'd had some time, and for me, he was the gospel when it came to her. The memories my father shared were colored by his anger, parsed out as if they were in short supply and he wanted to hold most of them for himself. Those TJ had were colored by the innocence of his youth, and I preferred the bright, beautiful Mama he remembered.

"She'd be so happy for you to have it," TJ had told me.

Now, looking at the tiny diamond glinting on Joey's finger, I thought maybe I felt Mama's approval, a faint acknowledgment from something beyond this earthly plane that this was right. I rolled my head to glance at Joey's pretty face, and found her watching me.

"What are you thinking about?" her voice was wary, as if she'd convinced herself I would change my mind.

I dropped a hand atop hers, loving the feel of the ring beneath my palm. "I'm happy. I was thinking how glad my mama would be to see you wearing her ring. I was just feeling..." I didn't have words to express the way I felt about Joey becoming my wife. It was like winning every championship game in the league without even having to try.

"You sure you don't have regrets?" Joey whispered.

I didn't like her uncertainty. "Do you?" I double-checked.

"Not about you, John. This thing with us? This feels right. I just want to make sure I haven't pushed you into something."

I rolled and took her in my arms, pulling her on top of me.

"It is right," I told her. I let my hands coast across her skin, cupping her perfect ass and holding her against me. She dropped her head to kiss me, and soon, her hands slid between us to notch me at her entrance. We hadn't used condoms since that first time because Joey had an IUD and she'd told me that she and Evan had used a condom every single time. Evidently, he had a very specific plan about children and was willing to sacrifice pleasure to make sure nothing happened ahead of schedule.

I thought if something happened, and Joey ended up pregnant with my baby that it would be the happiest accident in the whole world.

We met Mr. And Mrs. Baxter at the diner in Boomsmack, where they were already seated in a booth when we arrived.

"Good morning, darlin'," Mr. Baxter said, rising to take Joey's hand and kiss her cheek. "Son," he said, extending a hand for me to shake. He seemed to have accepted the situation overnight and I didn't sense any hostility from him. Mrs. Baxter was another story. She didn't greet either of us from her spot next to the window, just kept her hands tucked around her coffee cup and watched us sit down.

"Good morning, Mama," Joey said. "Did you sleep well?"

Mrs. Baxter scoffed. "Of course not."

I braced myself, ready for a new battle today, but Mrs. Baxter's eyes had fixed themselves to Joey's hand. To the ring.

"The jeweler was open early," Mrs. Baxter said, a note of something harsh in her voice. "On a Sunday."

Joey lifted her hand and displayed the ring, which shone in the morning light coming through the window. It was small, nothing like the one on Mrs. Baxter's hand. But it was beautiful and Joey's smile when she held it up was even more gorgeous.

"Well, look at that," Mr. Baxter said. "Honey, that's gorgeous."

"Thank you," Joey said, ignoring her mother's quip about the jeweler.

The waitress stopped by and took orders, and then we were left with the heaviness of the impending conversation. Joey's hand on my thigh beneath the table gave me the courage I needed to sit still, to take the scrutiny of this expectant couple. A couple who had actively worked to prevent us from ever being together, and one that had never accepted me. All of that aside, these were Joey's parents. If she needed to maintain a relationship with them, I wasn't going to let my own feelings get in the way. Nothing said I had to be golf buddies with Mr. Baxter.

"So tell us about your plans, pumpkin." Mr. Baxter

grinned over the rim of his coffee cup. "What have you been doing up here in Virginia since you left?"

I admired the man. His easygoing attitude appeared unflappable. He was intimidating in his stature and confidence about his place in the world, but unlike his wife, he didn't seem to want to wield his position like a spear.

"Well, there's the engagement, obviously," Joey shot a smile at me and I smiled back. "But I've also been shadowing a couple people—one at a biomedical company that works in animal health, and one in a government agency that tracks wildlife."

"Why?" Mrs. Baxter asked.

"Because, Mama. I want to work. I want to use my degree. I'm not interested in hosting garden parties and going to bridge club to talk about people with other ladies. I want to do something that matters."

"Joey, darlin', what your mama does matters," Mr. Baxter said in a somewhat stern tone, defending his wife who simply sniffed and looked hurt.

"That's not what I meant," Joey said, her hand on my thigh tightening for a brief moment as if drawing strength. "I just mean that it isn't what I want for me. I want to work. And I think I'm going to go to work for the biotech."

"So you plan to stay here?" Mrs. Baxter asked, her voice higher than before.

"Yes," Joey said, glancing at me. We hadn't even gotten to have this conversation yet, but I loved how confident she sounded as she explained what the company did. "And John's job is here, obviously," she added.

"And when will this wedding be?" Mrs. Baxter asked.

"We haven't even discussed it," Joey said. "There's no hurry."

The food arrived, and everyone was quiet, the preceding words circling the table. I ate my eggs, a surprising calm settling over me. Joey was here. She was staying.

This was what happy felt like.

"You'll have to write apology notes," Mrs. Baxter said with no preamble.

"What?" Joey asked, looking up from her pancakes.

"To every guest and vendor who went out of their way to attend your wedding to Evan."

"Okay," Joey agreed.

"I assume you've apologized to him?" she asked.

"Of course I have."

"His parents?"

"Er. Not yet," Joey's shoulders fell a bit.

"And does he know about... this?" Mrs. Baxter pointed at me with her fork. I had become "this."

Joey swung her gaze to me. "No. It just happened."

Mrs. Baxter's face settled into a stern expression. "I'll leave it to you to handle it all properly. I think you know you cannot in clear conscience embark on another wedding effort without properly handling the details of the last."

"Of course," Joey said.

For a moment, no one spoke, and the remnants of the conversation settled with the leftover bits of waffle and muffin on our plates. Then Mr. Baxter pushed his plate away and smiled broadly at me.

"So John, when does the season start again? I've never

really followed ice hockey, but I guess that's about to change."

I smiled back at him, happy to have something to talk about where I was the authority.

For the next half hour, we talked about the Wombats, about the league, and about my prospects. It felt good, being acknowledged by Mr. Baxter, even if Mrs. Baxter remained an icy presence at his side. Maybe one day, she'd come around. And if not, I didn't really care as long as Joey was on my side.

The Baxters departed that afternoon, after spending a little time at my house with us. Mrs. Baxter never really warmed up, though she did accept Hank climbing into her lap for a bit, which surprised me.

Eventually, they drove away, and Joey and I were left alone, facing each other as an engaged couple. I was about to sweep her into my arms and take her back to the bedroom when my phone vibrated in my pocket.

I pulled it out to see Coach Merit's name on the screen. The coach and I weren't exactly hang-out buddies, and a call from him was most likely news, and not necessarily good. My blood cooled in my veins. I was about to answer —should have answered—but Joey's eyes were burning with heat and her hands were at my waist, unfastening my jeans.

The phone was like a rock in my hand, threatening to

weigh me down despite the buoyant happiness I'd experienced all day with Joey at my side. As my fiancée.

"Do you need to get that?" Joey asked, stepping even closer and slipping her hand into my pants as a mischievous smile pulled her lips up to one side.

Her hand wrapped around me and my capacity for words was extinguished. I set the phone on the table in the foyer as Joey guided me down the hall, her hand starting a rhythm that every cell in my body burned to finish.

Our mouths fused as we fell onto my bed, and her hand left me only long enough to pull off her own clothes while I did the same. Every time I touched her, I marveled that she was really mine to hold, that my dreams were all coming true right here in my arms.

Joey climbed onto me, pushing me to lay back on the bed, and she slowly made her way down my torso, littering the path behind her with kisses and nips to my skin that had me clawing the covers for control. When her hot breath hit my penis, I lurched up, trying to take control, but she pressed me back down with a light laugh. "I'm in charge now, Sammy."

Her tongue made a slow swipe down my length, and then swirled around the head as stars exploded behind my eyes. Joey's mouth was taking me in, her wet heat surrounding me as her hands caressed my balls and I fought for control.

Puppies? No. Golf? Not working. Mrs. Baxter's disappointed frown. There it was... I pulled myself from the brink and let Joey work me, taking me deep down her throat and then sucking as she came off and did it over again.

"Oh god," I managed. "That is... That is..."

"Good?" she asked, her head popping up to look into my face.

"They haven't invented a word for it yet. Something way, way better than good."

She started again, one hand wrapped around my base while her mouth challenged every last bit of my willpower. Finally, I couldn't take it any more, and I hauled her up over me, barely in control as she sank down onto me and surrounded me with a totally different wet heat as her head dropped back.

"You feel so good," she moaned, moving slowly over me. Each undulation of her hips was sheer torture, if torture was something performed by the most beautiful woman you could imagine and designed to drive you wild with pleasure.

"So. Fucking. Good," she said, punctuating each word with a thrust.

I froze, my eyes popping open. "Did you just..."

She stopped moving, grinning at me. "I can curse. I know all the words."

"I've literally never heard you curse."

A wicked smile crossed her lips and her eyes glinted as she leaned down over me, her hair brushing my chest as her lips moved close to my ear. "Do you like it? Do you want me to talk dirty to you while I fuck you?"

Holy shit. Those words? From her mouth? I just about

lost it. "God, yes," I groaned. "But I won't last long if you do."

The wicked smile stayed in place, and she leaned up again. "John, I love feeling your cock filling me up like this." She thrust. "It's so fucking big, so good." She thrust again. "You're so good, it's like you were made just to fuck me." Her voice broke a little as she thrust that time, and my control began to slip from my grasp.

She moved over me, the words forgotten in pursuit of the pleasure, and when she moaned—a husky, desperate sound—my body released. All the tension coiled up in my spine, in my limbs, flew outward as I let go, forced to orgasm by Joey's utter perfection.

She matched me, still moving over me, her cries becoming higher and breathier, and then finally, stopping as she let herself collapse over my chest.

"Oh god," she whispered. "Wow. I think I like talking dirty."

"I know I like it when you do," I said.

"I think it was seeing what it did to you," she said turning her head and pushing her soft hair away from my face.

"Just looking at you turns me on," I told her, clasping her body to mine. "Hearing you say dirty things? That's almost too much. No man could survive it."

Her back vibrated with her laugh, and I held her there, reveling in the fact that I had everything I'd ever wanted right here in my arms. It was so fucking perfect I was afraid to move.

CHAPTER 20
JOEY

BACON SOLVES EVERYTHING

Monday morning felt like the start of a new lifetime, not just a new week. I rolled out of John's arms, out of bed and into a world where my life was my own, where decisions lay before me like flowers ready to be picked and arranged, and where I was the one in control.

I'd fallen asleep the night before early, tucking myself in and drifting off after kissing John goodnight in the kitchen and leaving him there. I was exhausted—it turns out that reclaiming your life from your family years beyond the point where you should have done it takes a lot of effort.

But it had been worth it.

I was free, and the ring gleaming on my hand felt more like a prism opening up bright new vistas ahead of me than like the shackle that Evan's ring had been.

In the kitchen, I made coffee and whipped up a couple omelets, putting one into the microwave to stay warm for John. And then I watched the clock. I had calls to make, but it wouldn't do to bombard anyone first thing on a Monday morning. I sat at the kitchen table with the laptop John had loaned me, and made a list.

1. Job. Call Elodie, interview? Call Tennessee and reject offer. Nicely.
2. Clothes. Talk Mama into shipping my things. Or plan to go pick them up. Road trip? Would Sammy want to go?
3. Call Clara to thank her.
4. Plan a wedding?

I wasn't sure about that last one. John had proposed. And I thought it was pretty close to a real proposal, at least for me. He'd said words I didn't think anyone else would ever improve upon, and I already knew it was pointless trying to fit any other man into the mold I'd made of him as the perfect guy.

But there was the small question of whether I'd pushed John into the whole thing. And whether he might one day resent me for it.

I was sitting with my chin in my hand, contemplating additional list items, when John appeared, walking toward the kitchen down the hallway to the back of the house. He looked adorably sleepy, his hair mussed and his face ruddy with dreams.

"Why'd you let me sleep so late?" he asked, but there was no venom in his voice.

"I thought you might need it. You were up late?" I

wasn't sure if he had been. I only knew he hadn't been in bed when I'd woken up to use the restroom around midnight. Maybe he'd come to bed and gotten up, unable to sleep?

"I was, yeah." He took the chair across from me, looking around as if he'd never seen his own kitchen before.

"Everything okay?" I asked. My stomach clenched. Something was wrong. I could feel it. Could he have been up late thinking about what a stupid idea it was to propose to me? Was he realizing that saving me had ruined his own life? I pushed the ring around on my finger as I waited for his answer.

His hand caught mine, righted the ring. "I'm so glad you're here," he said quietly. "That we got this time."

I squinted, trying to see past the worry lines on his face and to the heart of the matter. "Me too." Was he about to tell me it was all over?

I braced as his eyes met mine. "Do I smell bacon?"

Almost everything inside me relaxed. A reprieve. But was he only delaying telling me the truth?

"Yeah. I made you an omelet too."

"I would've proposed years ago if I'd known it would mean breakfast would be ready when I woke up every day," he joked, his face finally relaxing into the familiar expression I knew and loved.

"Don't get used to it," I told him, retrieving the plate from the microwave and setting it in front of him. "I'll be working soon, hopefully, and then might not have time for much beyond a cup of coffee and a kiss."

He raised an eyebrow and shot me a look that suggested

he was thinking exactly what I was—that kisses tended to lead to other things. Good things. Hot things.

"Thanks," he said, accepting the fork I handed him. I retook my seat across from him. "So work, huh?"

"I'm going to call Elodie at ten and ask if we can start exploring some of the openings she mentioned."

"Private sector, then," John said, a half-smile on his full lips.

"The work they're doing is so exciting and it has direct impacts on human medicine." The excitement I felt at the idea of finally doing the kind of work I'd always dreamed of threatened to bubble out of me.

"That's awesome," he said. "I'm proud of you."

I let the words sink in and then tumbled around in them for a moment—like a lottery winner rolling around in dollar bills. It was gratifying, and John's pride and support were everything I'd never gotten from my parents.

"Thanks," I said. It was almost ten and my hands were itching to make the call. John was busy eating the food in front of him, so I stood, carrying my phone to look out on the back yard while I dialed.

"Elodie Masters," Elodie answered.

"Hi there. It's Josephine Baxter. How are you?"

"Good, Josephine. How are you?"

"I'm great. Listen, I'm calling to see if you really think there might be a position there for me. I would love to talk more about any opportunities you know about."

"Your timing is amazing," she said, my heart surging as she spoke. "My lab assistant is leaving at the end of the week to move across the country because of a family issue.

You'd be a perfect replacement if that sounds interesting to you."

"Really?" I might have sounded a tiny bit too happy about what was potentially another person's misfortune. "I mean, I hope everything is okay."

"I don't suppose you'd be able to come in this week to learn the job from her and give her a chance to hand off?"

"This week?" I echoed, immediately wishing I sounded less surprised and more professional and polished. "Yeah, er. Yes, that could work."

"Really? That would be incredible."

I bounced on my toes as I waited for her to continue.

"We often do a probationary period when we bring in someone new. You'd get a good chance to really see the work you'd be doing in a condensed amount of time this week. I might be able to have the HR department write a contract with a shortened probation."

"Which would mean...?"

"Sorry. Yeah, I'm just excited that you're coming in. Not making myself clear. Once you're through probation, all the benefits kick in, like health insurance and your retirement savings and stock options."

"Stock options?" I asked, walking back to the table where I'd left the laptop, thinking maybe I should be writing this down. John's eyes met mine and widened when I said these words.

"Yes. They're a part of the compensation. There will also be a bunch of paperwork—the contract and the non-compete and all that good stuff. I can talk you through all of it, but I'll send over a preliminary offer this morning if you like. Just give me an hour or so to bribe the head of HR to fast-track it."

"Oh my gosh, that would be amazing."

"Josephine, I'm really glad you called."

"Me too. Thank you so much for the opportunity."

I hung up a different person than I'd been from when I'd picked up the phone. I was a different person than I'd been the day before. Or two weeks before.

"You got a job," John said, his voice holding something like awe.

"I got a job," I agreed.

He slid out of his chair and grabbed my hand, tugging me into a hug and then spinning me around. "I'm so proud of you, baby."

I buried my head in his shoulder, breathing in the familiar and comforting scent of my best friend, my fiancé, my soul mate. God, I hoped we were for real. I couldn't imagine life without him now that I'd found him.

But when I pulled back, his face still held a look I didn't know. I shook my head at him, waiting for my mind to piece together the expression, but nothing came. "I still feel like there's something wrong," I told him. "You promise everything's okay?"

The look vanished immediately and John beamed at me. "Promise. Nothing a trip to the gym can't fix."

"Ooh, yes. If we make it a quick one, I'll come," I told him. "I want to be back when my offer comes in."

"Let's take two cars," John suggested, that dark cloud dropping through his eyes again. "I'm probably going to be there a while, and then I've got to stop through the foundation offices and make sure everything is set for launch this week."

"Launch?" I asked.

"Hockey camp starts Wednesday," he said, but his face was grim, nothing like the smile it usually held when he talked about his foundation.

As we got ready and I followed his big black truck to the gym, I told myself that whatever was going on with him would solve itself. Or he'd work through it at the gym or the office. I hoped it was true, but something in my gut wasn't sitting right. I vowed to get to the bottom of it when he came home.

CHAPTER 21

JOHN

EVEN SWAG WON'T HELP

I'd gone to check messages after Joey fell asleep in my arms, and had ended up staying up late. Or early, depending on your perspective. The dark of the previous night had pressed in around me as I'd stewed over Coach Merit's message.

Now, as I packed plates onto the ends of the bar I was going to chest press into oblivion, his voice looped in my head.

...just hadn't planned on you starting so soon... veteran goalie... trading you...

I still couldn't make all the words line up in a way I could stomach.

Coach Merit wanted to trade me and was in talks with other teams about bringing in a more experienced goalie. I had a call in to Shotz, my agent, but hadn't heard back from him yet.

All I'd thought about since Mizzoni had been injured was how to fill his shoes. How to prove I could do it, that I was worthy. My teammates told me they had faith in me, the managers had said the same. Even Coach Merit had told me he thought I had what it took.

I was going to prove them all right by being the very best, cementing my place by making All Star. I was going to be a standout, and prove to everyone—most of all myself—that I deserved to be where I was.

Only now it was pretty clear I'd been wrong. Coach didn't think I could hold up. He was worried I'd blow the team's chances.

I threw the last plate on the bar and slammed my index finger between it and the previous one. Dammit. The pain that shot through my hand couldn't compete with the one in my heart, though.

For a long moment, I stood still, my eyes closed, and my hand curled against my chest. And it wasn't the coach's voice I heard. It was Dad's.

...should never have agreed when your mom said she wanted another baby... ended up with you... not half the athlete your brother will be...

He'd stopped these kinds of taunts when I'd gotten MVP in high school, once I'd been old enough to get myself to practice and pay for gear on my own. Once my life stopped impacting his. But fuck if the things he'd said when I was a kid didn't still hurt.

I cringed, imagining telling him I was being traded.

"Hey." A soft voice came from behind me, and a second later Joey's arms slipped around my waist.

I opened my eyes and let her warmth sink into my back for a minute before spinning around to look at her. She'd pulled out one air pod and wore a concerned look, her brows low over her expressive eyes.

"What's wrong, John?"

"I'm fine, baby." I couldn't tell her. Not yet. Not when everything in her life was finally going the way she wanted it to. Why did her happy day have to coincide with my awful one? I was determined not to let my shadow fall over her joy. Not yet.

"Did you hurt your hand?" she asked, pulling it away from my chest.

"Just pinched my fingers." We both looked down at my swelling index finger. "It'll be okay."

Joey bent her head and kissed my finger, then smiled up at me, the uncertainty still in her gaze. She knew something was wrong, but she wasn't going to force it. God, I loved her.

"Hey, will you spot me for a second?" Joey gestured to a bench with a barbell resting above it. "I'm going for a personal record," she said.

"That's a lot of weight, baby."

She raised an eyebrow and cocked a hip. "You saying I can't do it?"

I shook my head and laughed. Joey had taken to strength training like she took to everything—with gusto and impressive dedication. And the body that was emerging along with her confidence was so fucking sexy. The confidence even more so than the muscles, but I loved it all.

I positioned myself above her as she lay on her back and tested the weight. Gently, I helped her move it off the rack and kept my hands ready as she lowered it slowly and then began to press it back up. She faltered for a moment, and I had to keep myself from rescuing her. I wouldn't do it for a dude, I reminded myself, not unless he really needed me to. Her arms shook, and her face reddened, but she muscled the bar back up, and then met my eyes. I closed my hands around it and helped her re-rack it, elation shooting through me as she sat up smiling.

"You did it."

"Of course I did," she said, grinning. "I have the best trainer in town."

"Good job, baby." I was so proud of her, so proud of the person she'd always been and even more excited to see the one she would be as she moved more fully into this version of her life.

Only... I didn't think I'd be here to see it. God only knew where I'd be. But it didn't seem like I was going to get to stay in Wilcox.

I moved to my own rack and powered through the last few sets of my workout, my mind not in it. And then I kissed Joey goodbye and headed for the office.

"Boss," Anthony said, greeting me from his desk in the corner of the wide open room we used as office, shipping center, and meeting facility for the Futures on Ice Foundation.

"Hey Anthony," I said, working to put a bit of cheer into my voice. "How's everything looking?"

"Waiting for the shoe to drop," he said.

I took a chair at the desk I usually used when I stopped in. "What does that mean?"

"It means everything is going according to plan, no vendors have dropped, the caterers are all set for lunches, and not a single camper has cancelled."

"Wow." That was pretty incredible. It was only the second year we'd been running the camp, and the year prior it felt like if something could go wrong, it did. "That's great."

"The rink confirmed our time slots this morning, and we've got the coaches coming in later for our final prep meeting."

"Players confirmed?" I had a bunch of the Wombats skating a demo on the last day of camp.

"All in," Anthony said.

I sighed. I'd almost been hoping there would be some kind of emergency for me to handle, something that needed doing. But Anthony was a one-man show—totally capable. With the oversight of the board and the funding provided by local businesses and a couple grants, it was all running smoothly.

I'd had plans to apply for another grant that would allow me to run a second session nearby in Richmond, but it looked like that might fall apart now too. If I wasn't going to be here, what was the point?

"Can I do anything?" I asked him now. "Sort welcome packs? Put together the swag bags?"

"Oh yeah, you could do that," he said, nodding to the corner where boxes were piled. "I haven't gotten there yet."

"Consider it done." Opening boxes and assembling the packs of swag the campers would take with them was the perfect mindless activity. It allowed my head to roam freely over the coach's message and think about how I was going to tell Joey.

Of course first, I needed to actually talk to the coach, which I wasn't looking forward to doing.

When there was nothing left for me to micromanage at the office, I went back out to my truck and dialed Coach Merit.

"Samuels," he said in the stern, serious voice I'd grown used to.

"Hey Coach. Got your message." I didn't pretend to be happy about it. He wouldn't care.

"Yeah," he said, and I heard him take a deep breath. "Not an easy decision, John. But we really thought you'd have another year under Mizzoni."

"Yeah."

"And while I have no doubt about your talent, we've got to think about your experience. There are gonna be situations where sheer time in the game will make the difference."

"Sure."

"And I need to think about the team as a whole."

"Yeah." I let my eyes drift shut, exhausted by the thought of settling in at yet another team, being the new guy again. I'd taken a lot of shit from Mizzoni, and had finally come to an understanding with him, and been able to rely on his mentorship. I wasn't excited about doing it all again. I wanted to start. And I thought I could. But it wasn't my opinion that mattered.

"I'm not saying anything to the other guys yet," Coach was saying. "Still feeling things out. I just wanted to give you the heads up, so you'd be ready. I'm talking to Shotz too. He'll get you a good deal, don't worry."

"Okay." I should have asked who he was looking at, where he thought I might go, but I didn't have the energy.

"I'll be in touch."

"Okay, thanks Coach."

We hung up and I let the reality of the situation worm through my veins, worked to accept it. I couldn't control it. I couldn't change it. I would have to figure out how to be okay with it.

It just seemed like my whole life had been full of situations like this. Things I couldn't control but would have to accept.

I drove to the rink, needing to get some ice under my skates to try to even out my thinking before I went home to Joey.

As I made lazy turns around the rink, I let my mind roll. Would she consider coming with me? But Joey didn't want to be a hockey wife. She hadn't sought me out in hopes of a puck bunny lifestyle. She'd come to me because of our history. But would our history be enough to survive long distance immediately after finding one another? It wasn't what I wanted. Not at all.

Shotz called as I skated, and I moved to the edge of the ice to talk to him. He said all the expected things—that this could be really good for me, that my season with the Wombats meant a stronger contract with the next team. But he didn't suggest there was a way I could just...stay.

Eventually, I packed up and headed home. Even though I wasn't excited to tell Joey what I knew, I was excited to hear her news. And to see her again, to hold her close to me and breathe her in.

I parked the truck and headed inside, each tense muscle in my body loosening slightly with each step I got closer to Joey.

"Hey, you," she said, turning from the couch where she was sitting with a glass of wine when I walked through the door. Hank sat behind her, his paws buried in her bright blond hair.

"Hey baby," I said. I stepped close and gave Hank a scratch between the ears and leaned over to kiss Joey's forehead.

"Want to join me for a glass of wine? I made some dinner, too, but it'll keep."

"That sounds amazing," I told her, heading into the kitchen where the bottle of shiraz was open on the counter. I poured a glass and then moved back to join Joey on the couch. "So. Tell me everything."

Joey's smile widened and her eyes did the same, as if there was so much good stuff in her mind it was all trying to come out at once. "Well," she said, "I'm the new lab assistant at FarmPharma Biologic."

"You accepted the offer?" My heart swelled with happiness for her. She looked so proud, her eyes beaming as her cheeks turned pink.

She nodded and I held my glass out to her. After a quick clink, she dove into details. "The pay is... well, it's way better than I expected for an entry level job, but the best part is that I'll be working directly with Dr. Masters, who is so ridiculously amazing. John, I'm going to learn so much."

"That's amazing. When do you start?"

"I'm going in for the rest of this week to learn the ropes from the lab assistant who is leaving, and then I'll start officially next week."

"So quick," I commented.

"Right," she said. "So I need to figure some things out, I guess. Like clothes for work, and a computer of my own..." I could almost see gears turning behind Joey's eyes.

"Did your dad reinstate your access to money?"

She nodded, but her look was uncertain. "Only, I don't want it. You know? I want to do this on my own."

"I get it," I said, proud of her again.

"So I wondered..." Joey hesitated. "Do you think I could take out a loan from you? Just until I get my first paycheck?"

"No."

"No?"

"If we're getting married, what's mine is yours anyway. Why don't I just get you a credit card?"

She shook her head so violently Hank leapt off the couch and wandered around to my feet, looking offended. "The whole point is to be independent, John."

"Okay, then yes. You can take out a loan. I'll give you my card, and we can just keep track of what you spend." It was silly, but if it made her feel better, it was fine.

"Thank you," she said, beaming at me. "And how was your day? Is the camp all ready to launch Wednesday?"

It touched me that she knew my plans for the week and seemed to sense how important the camp was to me. "Everything looks good," I told her.

"So now are you going to tell me what's bothering you?"

Not only did she know what was important to me, but she read me so well she knew when something was wrong.

I didn't think I could hide it from her much longer, so I settled back, took a long sip of wine, and braced myself to tell her the truth.

CHAPTER 22
JOEY

FRIENDS AND MAGIC

"Trade?" I asked, my voice higher than intended. It seemed like all the chaos in my own life was finally tapering off, and now this?

John's face was drawn and pale, and his beautiful dark eyes looked dull. This news had stolen his shine, and it made me want to rush over to the coach's house and shake some sense into the guy.

"Where will they send you?" I asked. "Why would they want to trade you, though?" I didn't understand. He was so talented, and I'd seen how much the fans loved him when we'd been at Paddy's that night. "But you're the youngest goalie in the league!" I repeated the fact I'd heard so many times.

"That's why," he said. "I don't have the experience a lot of other guys have, which means I might make poor decisions when the heat is on, just because so many things will be new to me. They don't want a guy to be living through a bunch of first times with their team. They want a vet, someone who's already proven."

"That's not fair," I said. "This is your time to get that experience."

"Yeah, but they thought I'd be getting it with Mizzoni there to take over when I screw up."

"So they should bring in a second string." I knew next to nothing about hockey and sensed that this wasn't a solution, but I was grasping at straws.

"My agent says this isn't surprising."

"Can't he fight for you to stay?"

"He said he'd try, but he thinks he can leverage my success at the end of last season to get me better contract terms somewhere else. He thinks it's a good idea."

"So you'll have to move?" I asked, realizing the full implications of this news. If he moved, I should move. We were a couple. But I'd just gotten my dream job. My life was just starting, and it was here... in Wilcox.

"Unless the team is in commuting distance. Like if it was DC, I guess I could come home sometimes when we had a few days off."

His voice mirrored the disdain I felt for this idea. I'd never see him. We'd be apart more than we were together.

"I could look for another job," I said, trying to rally excitement for this idea, but realizing I really couldn't. I'd signed a non-compete. I couldn't work for a biotech company for a year after concluding my employment with FarmPharma. I looked. For other ideas. "I could see if maybe my job could be remote."

"Don't you work like, in a lab? With microscopes and things?" John asked. "How would you do that from home?"

"Maybe I could like, process data or something instead," I said.

"Joey," Sammy took my face in his hands and kissed the tip of my nose. "That's not what you want and there is no way I'm going to let you compromise your own future for mine."

"There are a lot of biotech companies out west," I said after that. "I could work here for now but start interviewing and stuff..."

"No." John sat up, putting his wine on the coffee table. "Look, whatever happens, you should stay here, in this house. It's a great commute for you from here, and this will still be our home, okay?"

"Not if you aren't here," I said, feeling on the verge of tears.

"Well, we don't know anything yet," he said, but his voice was clear. Something was happening, and it wasn't going to be good.

"I hate this," I told him, moving to nestle myself against him. His arms fell around me automatically, and I realized I didn't want to be without him. Not when I'd just found him again.

"We'll figure it out," he said. And then he looked deep into my eyes, and the need and sadness I saw there nearly broke my heart.

I leaned my head up and kissed him. I couldn't undo what had been done, but I could prove that we were okay, solid. I kissed him with all the reassurance and love I could find inside myself, doing my best to tell him I'd be here either way. I was not going to let this ruin what we'd only just discovered again.

I started work for real the next day.

I loved everything about it. From leaving the house in the morning in my "business clothes" to parking outside the long, low building near the FarmPharma sign and feeling a misplaced sense of pride that I was part of this. Part of something.

It would wear off, I was sure. But I reveled in the moment when the woman from HR walked me out to my cubicle, and nearly did a little fist pump when Dr. Masters gave me my own lab coat. It was like being a kid, playing at "job." Except it was all real.

The elation was tempered by the little worry in the back of my mind that kept reminding me that in the face of my joy, John was suffering. His camp launched tomorrow, and I knew he was worried about keeping his focus for the kids. But so much of that camp was based on who he was, who he'd been, and how he'd gotten to where he was. And now it was being threatened.

My real worry about John's trade was selfish.

The ring on my finger caught the fluorescent lights overhead in the lab, and the sparkle I saw matched the flicker I felt inside at the idea of marrying my best friend.

I spent the day shadowing Virginia, the woman who

was leaving, and there wasn't a moment when I regretted leaving my past behind and taking this step through the door to my future.

"My daughter had another grand baby," Virginia told me over sandwiches in the lounge at lunchtime. John had made mine—ham and cheese—and he'd tucked in a little note wishing me good luck. "I've been out to visit the other two, but now my oldest grandkid is almost five, and I just feel like I'm missing everything. That's why I'm moving to be with them."

Virginia did not look old enough to be a grandmother, and I told her so, hoping that wasn't the wrong thing to say.

"I appreciate the compliment," she said, her face aglow beneath the dark hair she'd pulled back into a bun. "But what you're looking at here is a very late bloomer, I guess."

"What do you mean?" I asked.

"I got married young. Like way too young."

I felt every one of my twenty-three years at that moment. "How young?"

"Eighteen," she said with a laugh. "Married my high school sweetheart." She shook her head, as if she was looking back into the past and laughing at her younger self. "Those things never work out, do they?"

"Maybe," I said, the sandwich beginning to feel like it wasn't settling quite right.

"Well, it was the wrong move for me," she went on. "I had babies at twenty and twenty-two, and spent the rest of my youth chasing them around. Not that I regret a second of that. It was hard, though. Our lives weren't formed when we got together and they began to diverge as we aged and figured out what we each wanted. We got divorced when I was twenty-four, and I worked hard to raise those kids right—to give them things I didn't get."

I nibbled the cookie John had included in my lunch and listened, my heart doing strange things in my chest. Why was it I couldn't just hear someone's story without having to see myself in every aspect of it?

"I went to night school to get my degree," she went on. "And when they were in high school, I started work. And then I met Elodie."

"She's great," I said, already knowing it was true.

"She's one in a million," Virginia confirmed. "And she has a knack for hiring exactly the right people. Which says a lot about you."

"Thanks."

"So..." Virginia raised her eyebrows at me. "Don't make me be nosey. Just tell me."

"Tell you what?"

"Everyone has a story. Everyone has the thing that's top of mind at a particular moment. Mine is grandkids and a move to California. Yours is a brand new job and an engagement ring?"

"You nailed it." I considered how much I wanted to tell her, and realized I was excited to talk about all of it. I didn't have a lot of friends here yet. There was Clara, of course. But now that the chance to talk to someone about John had popped up, I found myself eager to open my mouth. "I'm getting married. But he's not my high school sweetheart. He's my high school best friend. Do you think that has better odds?"

Virginia's eyes were warm. "Friends make the very best partners," she said. "As long as you've got a little magic too."

"Oh, we've got plenty of magic."

"Good," she said, dropping her cheek into her hand and giving me a misty smile. "Because when the romance wears off, you'll have friendship to sustain you. And then hopefully, when you really need it, you'll get the magic."

"I hope so," I told her, finishing my cookie. I felt like maybe we could use a little magic right now.

CHAPTER 23
JOHN

THE ART OF ICE CLEANING

"First of all, I want to thank each and every one of you for coming here to spend the rest of this week with me," I practically screamed to be heard, addressing the squirming crowd of boys and girls gathered in the family lounge at the Wilcox rink. "I know it's not always easy to figure out all the details, and so I also need to say thank you to all the parents who made it happen to get you here."

A group of parents stood around the perimeter of the room, many of them looking like they had other places they wanted or needed to be.

"We'll take good care of your kids between the hours of eight-thirty and five-thirty," I went on. "And also for every minute after that. Because once you've been a Wombat, you're a Wombat for life."

A few of the kids cheered at this proclamation.

I'd given the speech last year too, and both times that particular line had felt somewhat hollow. Last year, I hadn't been sure if I'd keep my position on the team—Mizzoni seemed so opposed to having me around. This year... well, it seemed like I wasn't destined to be a Wombat much longer. But these kids would always have the experience of being Junior Wombats, of training in a real FHL rink, of meeting their idols, and of being shown one example of what was possible, despite whatever circumstances they faced.

There were some parents here, but most of these kids came from homes where work was a priority, not a luxury. Most of these kids came from homes that couldn't afford summer camps, which was why the grants we operated with were so critical. The kids didn't pay a dime to come, and it was part of my mission to make sure they never felt like anything we gave them was charity.

"All right, Wombats," I said, raising my voice again. "I want to make sure everyone here knows the rules."

"Rules?" one of the kids said, sounding disappointed.

"Yep. Rules. Number one. You respect everyone else here. You can have fun, you can joke and you can tease, but all of it happens in an environment of respect. We lift each other up. If someone needs a hand, you give it to them, and know that they'll be there to do the same for you. This place runs on respect. That's how it is on the team I play for, and that's how it will be for you. Can you guys tell me rule one?"

"RESPECT!" the kids called back.

"Good. Rule two. Everyone here is a Wombat. There is no ranking. We're all here to learn and practice, get better and have fun. I don't want to hear talk about who's better than who. That's not what we're about. So, can I hear you tell me rule two?"

"All Wombats!"

"Right. And finally, rule three. Fun. We will have fun. What's rule three?"

They had no trouble with that one at all.

"Great. Let's get going," I told them. "Hit the benches outside and get your skates on. No one on the ice yet, okay?"

The room erupted in chaos, and a few minutes later the kids had gone out to meet Julius Ramon, Sly, and Rock Stevens, who were helping with the first half of day one. And I was left alone with the parents who hadn't felt comfortable just dropping their kids off.

"What can I tell you guys?" I asked them. "Any questions?"

There were a few standard questions about skill levels and what we'd be doing, and logistical concerns since some of our activities happened in places besides the rink. Once those had all been handled, a couple of the dads stood by.

"What else can I answer for you?" I asked them.

"Just curious about the team," one of them said. He wore coveralls with the name James printed at his chest. "You're taking Mizzoni's place, right?"

"Up to the coaches and managers," I said, hoping these guys didn't ask anything else and desperately wishing it was just my place.

"So that's a yes?" the guy next to James asked.

"I hope so," I said.

"Not instilling confidence, Samuels," James said. "You've

already shown your potential. This town is behind you. What else is there?"

As good as that felt, I knew it didn't really matter. "I really appreciate that," I told him. "This week, my only focus is on your kids. And after camp, we'll see what the team decides."

The two men looked at one another, exchanging frowns. "All right," James said, reaching out to shake my hand.

"This camp means a lot," the other guy told me. "My kid's been talking about it for months. Thanks."

"I hope he has a good experience," I said honestly. "I'll see you guys later."

The men left and I took a big breath, steadying myself to face the chaos. When I arrived out to where the kids all had their skates on, I was shocked to see them sitting quietly, Julius Ramon discussing all the different types of ice cleaning machines.

"Together, the lot of these devices are referred to as Zambonis," he was saying. "But it is critical to know that the word Zamboni is a registered trademark of the Zamboni Company. The machine we use here at the Wombats rink is not a Zamboni. But it is an excellent ice-cleaning machine, and whoever does the best job following your coach's directions today will get a ride on it before you go home."

Rock Stevens stood to one side of Ramon, his eyes drooping as his head began to nod over his chest. If he fell asleep on his feet, he could topple over and take out a few of these kids, so I needed to liven things up right away.

"Okay!" I clapped my hands and Stevens jumped.

"I'm awake!" he yelled.

The kids all laughed.

"How many of you guys have been on the ice before?" Our camp was open to all levels, so we had hockey players and total beginners alike.

Most of the hands shot up.

"Great. You guys head on out there." Kids got to their feet and after a lot of excessive clunking and shouting, we soon had a small army of skaters out on the ice with Julius and Sly. About five of the campers sat still, looking forlorn. These were my very favorite campers—the ones who would start out unsure, uncertain of their abilities, and who would undoubtedly discover something new inside them-selves this week. Something they would keep with them forever.

"Okay, now you guys get a choice. You can hear more about the Zamboni, or you can have a personal skating lesson from one of the best centers in the FHL, Rock Stevens."

"Rock!" the kids called out.

"That's right," Rock said, stepping forward. "All right, pee wee wombats. Let's go rock it!"

I headed out to the first group to join Julius who was setting up the first drill, while Rock ushered his crew out slowly, giving them each a PVC cage to push ahead of them.

And for the next ten hours, my heart was full, and the word "trade" didn't cross my mind. Not more than ten or fifteen thousand times.

Friday was the last day of camp. It was also the conclu-sion of Joey's first week at work and the end of her probationary period with the company, so I wanted to do something special.

I was floating on a high after a successful week, and having come home every night to an ecstatic Joey, who'd finally realized her own worth and was making all her dreams come true. It had been a good week.

Which was why I'd almost declined the call coming in from Coach Merit.

"Samuels?"

I regretted answering the call as I finished cleaning up the last drill from camp. All the campers had gotten their goodie bags and headed out for the night. It was late, but I'd asked Joey not to eat without me.

"Hey Coach."

"How was camp?" he asked. The camp had become a full-team effort, and while I knew the coach was aware of it and approved, I didn't know he especially cared.

"Went really well," I said. "The kids were great. Got a couple future FHL stars, I think."

"That's good, man."

I braced myself as he took an audible breath.

"So I have a bit of news about your trade."

I sank into a seat as Julius waved to me from the far side of the rink. He was headed out. I lifted a hand and let my eyes drift shut. I didn't want to hear this news.

"I've been talking to Shotz and to a few other organizations."

I knew Shotz would look out for me in negotiations, but I didn't think anyone could really get me what I wanted, which was to just stay here.

"Okay," I said, doing my best to buoy my heart and hopes.

"So it's between the Seattle Octopi and the Phoenix Firebirds."

West Coast. I was going to the West Coast. So much for the idea that I might be somewhat local. I'd have to move. What would happen to me and Joey?

"And right now, the Octopi seem pretty motivated. Either way, you'd need to be getting out there within the month."

I knew exactly who they'd be trading me for, then. Both of their second strings were vets. Young, but experienced. And both were waiting anxiously for a chance to start.

"Okay," I said again, my heart sinking inside me like an anchor.

"This is a good thing," Coach said. "It'll get you the experience you need. You're on track to be one of the best, son."

"Thanks."

"I know this isn't what you wanted."

"It's not." I could at least be honest with him.

"But it'll be the best thing in the end," he said.

There was nothing I could say to that, so I kept my mouth shut.

"I'll give you an update as soon as I've got it."

"Right."

"Proud of you, John."

"Thanks." I hung up, wondering exactly what the coach was proud of. That I was taking this without a fight? That I was willing to give up everything I'd found because I had no choice? Not much to be proud about in my estimation.

For a little while I just sat, staring out into the rink that I'd thought held my future. I let my eyes drift over the pristine white surface, track the blue and red lines, and finally come to rest on the net where I thought I'd been earning my place here.

Not good enough.

You were right, Dad. You've always been right.

INTERLUDE

JULIUS RAMON

I may have gotten carried away in my discussion of ice cleaning machines.

CHAPTER 24
JOEY

DONUTS. JUST IN CASE.

It had been a long week. But not because work at the lab was anything less than completely perfect.

It was long because John was so unhappy.

And that made me unhappy.

And I'd be damned if I was going to sit around and do nothing about it. The only problem was that there was very little I could actually do.

But I was trying. I heard the garage door rolling open late Friday evening, and shut the laptop in my room. "Clara, John's back. I need to go." I held the phone to my ear as I moved into the living room.

"Okay. Don't worry about this. I'm on it," she said.

I didn't know what Clara could do either, but I figured she might have an idea or two I hadn't thought of. Since I'd thought of...none.

Together we'd come up with a few shots in the dark, but I had the sense that my efforts to keep John with the Wombats were nothing more than a way to keep my disappointed mind busy. The reality was that my perfect future had lasted all of a few days before exploding.

I was on the couch with a glass of wine when John came in. I braced myself for a frown, but what appeared was something very different.

An enormous vase of lilies came through the door, blocking any traces of my fiancé from view. It was the largest arrangement of flowers I'd ever seen, and by far the most beautiful.

"Congratulations," he called, his voice muffled slightly by the flowers in his arms.

"Oh my gosh, those are amazing."

"Wait till you see what else I got," he said, moving to put the vase on the coffee table.

I bounced on the sofa. "What else?"

"Hold on," he said, grinning at me and dropping a quick kiss onto my forehead as he rushed by again, heading back out to the garage.

A moment later he reappeared, his hands full of food boxes and the smell of garlic preceding him. From one hand dangled a white paper bag.

"Food," I murmured appreciatively.

"Not just food," he corrected, coming to the couch to put these items with the flowers on the table. "Benito's Italian. Mizzoni and his uncle Julius say it's the most authentic and amazing they've tasted in the state."

"Well, okay then," I laughed.

"And I got donuts just in case."

"In case what?" I asked, loving the easy smile on his face as he dropped into the seat next to me.

"In case of emergency. Donuts are always good to have on hand. In case of whatever."

Laughter escaped from my lips, bubbling naturally from inside me without me thinking about it. John had this effect on me. He made me so happy that I didn't even think about being happy. He made the whole world around me feel happy too—his simple presence just made things better.

"Thank you for all this," I told him, leaning in to kiss his cheek. "The flowers are gorgeous."

"You're welcome. I'm so proud of you," he said, one hand brushing my cheek.

"How was camp?" I asked. "Did it all finish up well?"

He nodded. "Yeah, I think it did. The kids were so happy with their gifts, and when the Wombats skated for them, you would have thought they were meeting movie stars or superheroes."

"You guys are superheroes to kids who are into hockey," I reminded him. "And even if they're too young to realize it, you really are a superhero to them. Those kids wouldn't get a chance like this without you."

John lifted a shoulder, and I watched the clouds race through his eyes—the worry he'd been trying to hide from me all week.

We were both pretending everything was fine, even though it wasn't.

"I got some news too," he said, his voice losing its glee.

"Yeah?" I took a bite of the ravioli he'd brought me. Incredible.

"Looks like it's between Seattle and Phoenix."

My heart crumpled and the pasta in my mouth turned to paper. "Oh."

"Yeah."

I didn't know what to say. I wanted to paint a sunny picture, to tell him it would all be okay. But how could it be? John was going to leave. And neither of us could predict what that would mean for us.

"Maybe it—"

"You know what?" he asked, cutting me off.

"What?"

"For tonight, can we just pretend? Let's just pretend it isn't happening. Let's just pretend we don't know."

"Okay, Sammy," I said. "But I think it's good you got those donuts."

He nodded, and we ate pasta side by side on his couch, both of us doing our best to pretend and both of us failing miserably. Eventually, we were eating donuts, the feeling of our limited time together swaying over us like a pendulum.

There was a tiny spark of hope within me, based on some of the ideas Clara had come up with earlier, but I didn't have the local knowledge or resources to make things happen. Clara, however, had grown up here. So when John reached for me, pulling me into his lap on the couch, I let my mind go. I gave up my obsessive replaying of all the things I couldn't control and decided to put my faith in Clara and her contacts.

"Don't worry," she'd told me. "It isn't over yet."

I straddled John on the couch and let myself focus on those deep dark eyes, on the way he relaxed beneath my fingers as I kissed him softly, pushed my hands into his hair. I let myself sink onto him, keeping us each concentrated on the connection between us, the way our bodies fit and the peace we found in the aftermath when his arms circled my body, when our breathing was mirrored, when we were as connected as two people could be.

Nothing could break this, could it?

It was dark outside and the food had been reduced to crumbs, the bottle of wine empty when John said softly, "Joey. No matter what happens... these have been the best weeks of my life."

I was stone-cold sober and one hundred percent awake then. "Don't do that."

"I'm just—"

"You're telling me goodbye. You're giving up."

"No, I'm not. I just—"

I shook my head and blocked my ears like a child. "I'm not listening. I'm not hearing it, John. This isn't over."

"Cute," he said, pulling one hand from my head as I sagged next to him on the couch. "But this is out of our control."

"No." I disagreed. "My whole life so far has been about other people deciding my future. It's been about me going along with everything, not rocking the boat, and definitely not making any uncomfortable proclamations about what I might or might not actually want." My voice had risen as I spoke, and Hank padded out from the hallway now, clearly wondering what all the commotion was about. He leapt onto the coffee table, giving us a glance before moving to the vase and lifting a paw toward one lily.

"Hank, no," John warned.

Hank glanced at him and lowered his paw, playing innocent but not moving away from the flowers.

Then John turned to me. "I get it," he said, his voice full of exhaustion and defeat. "But this is hockey. I'm just a commodity right now. A warm body to fill a certain space. It takes years to be a name, to be the kind of player who gets to write his own ticket."

"Maybe," I said. "But I'm still not taking this lying down."

John raised an eyebrow. "Well, you may not wanna lay down, but I don't sleep well upright. I'm gonna go to bed."

"You know what I meant."

"Goodnight, baby."

"I might stay up a bit," I told him. I was too buzzed from the wine, my first week at work, and the desperate hope that Clara could really do magic to sleep yet.

"I'll see you in the morning."

"Leg day," I reminded him.

He rolled his eyes. "What have I created?"

That night I stayed up for hours, digging through websites and looking for leads. By the time I finally put my head down, I'd compiled everything for Clara and sent it in an email. It might not work, but at least I'd know I had given it my very best effort.

CHAPTER 25
JOHN

THERE'S A WRONG WAY TO BREAK UP

Joey was up half the night, and I understood why she was amped up. She'd just gotten so much of what she wanted, what she'd been working for. She was evolving before my eyes, morphing into this determined and independent strong woman—the completely grown-up version of the girl I'd loved in high school. And god, I loved her so much now it hurt.

And in parallel to her triumphs, I felt like I was shrinking, losing a grip on everything I thought I'd had, everything I thought I'd been.

We did leg day, and even my muscle strength seemed to be leaving me. I said goodbye to Joey after the gym, heading to the rink for an informal scrimmage Sly had called this morning. And for the first time in a long time, I didn't want to put on my skates either.

I knew I should be grateful any team wanted me. Whether it was Seattle or Phoenix, they were good teams full of great players. I'd learn. I'd grow.

And god, I'd miss Joey and the life we'd only begun to build here.

My body was leaden and my mood dark when I arrived at the rink. The team was there, and we played for a couple hours. If I'd been hoping to demonstrate all the reasons why they should hang on to me, I failed miserably. I let four goals past me and couldn't seem to keep my mind in the game at all.

The guys were strangely quiet about my poor performance. Where they'd normally at least give me shit for it, today they called out encouragement and kind words. Everyone knew about the trade, I realized.

I'd hit rock bottom. They were giving me their pity—the last thing I wanted.

"Samuels," Sly called as I shouldered my bag and headed for the door.

"Yeah?"

"Gonna need you Thursday night for a parade down Main Street."

I turned to face him, my bag sliding to the floor. "What?"

"You heard me. Parade."

That didn't make sense. We didn't do pre-season parades. "What? Why?"

He lifted a shoulder and made a face. "Some kind of goodwill thing. Just found out about it. We'll meet here and ride on the back of the flatbed Julius is hooking up. The town wants to celebrate their team."

Great. That was all I needed. One more reminder that I was no longer a part of the team, only this one would be painfully public. "Yeah, okay."

"Five o'clock here."

"Yeah."

As I climbed back up into my truck, my phone rang.

I sank into my seat and answered. "Coach."

"Seattle, John. Get out there next week. They've got someone getting in touch to make arrangements with you."

"Yeah. Okay."

"And John?" The coach's voice sounded far away, like he was talking through a tube from the other side of the world. "I'm sorry about this, son. It's not the way I would've had things go, but the owner has to do what's best for the team."

"I know." I did. I knew Coach Merit had little to do with the situation—he didn't decide who was coming or going. Those decisions came from higher up, which is why Sly had been acting so friendly the last few days. He was part of the management team now, and he'd probably known about this way before I did.

It hurt. There was no way to look at it and not feel like someone didn't want me.

I stared at the phone in my hand, wishing there was someone I could call who could make me feel slightly better, give me some better way to look at it. There was one person...

"TJ," I said when my brother answered.

"Hey little bro," he said. "How's life?"

I sighed. And then I told my brother everything. I told him about Joey and then about the trade, about the engagement and about how I was utterly and completely fucked. And how Dad had been right.

"First off, congratulations!" he said. "You've been in love

with that girl your whole life. Bout time she came around." His voice was full of happiness.

"Maybe you missed the other part about how I'm getting traded?"

"Yeah, I heard that. Just doesn't seem like big news compared to the first thing."

"Well the first thing is probably off thanks to the second thing."

"Why? You think you'll meet someone better in Seattle?"

"What? No. You're missing the point. I'm moving."

"Yeah, that's inconvenient, bro."

"So it's over."

"Only if that's what you want. I've heard they have these things called planes. Look into that."

"Once the season starts, I'm not going to have a lot of time for leisure trips, Teej. I'll be traveling and practicing, and that's it."

"For nine months, yeah."

"Yeah."

"Lemme ask you a question," he said. "You hadn't seen Joey in how long when she showed up in Wilcox?"

"Five years at least."

"But when she showed up, you just picked things up where you left off?"

"I mean, kind of."

"But you don't think you can handle nine months?"

"Things are different now."

"Yeah, now you've made a commitment to each other that means something. You gave her Mama's ring. She'll wait."

"It's not like I'd be moving back here after nine months. If I came back, it would only be for a visit."

"Look, Johnny. I get it. This isn't ideal. But it's also way better than what a lot of people get out of life. You found each other. You're in love. You're a fucking pro hockey player, and there's a kickass team that wants you. Maybe it's not the Wombats, but guess what? That's okay. And Joey? Don't forget I know that girl. She loves you, man. It'll work out."

"How'd you end up such an optimist?"

"What, you mean growing up with Dad?" TJ chuckled. Dad had been the complete opposite for my entire life. "He's mellowed a little, you know."

"I do not know."

"You should call him."

"Nah." That was the last thing I needed—to hear Dad's opinion on everything.

"I think being engaged just agrees with me. That, and I'm happy for you. You and Joey—that just makes sense to me. It'll work out."

"Maybe."

"Hey, I gotta run. Keep me informed and good luck, man. Love you."

"Love you."

I hung up and stared out the windshield at the Wombat's rink—the place I'd thought would be my second home for years. It hurt. All of it hurt. I didn't want to leave. But the choice wasn't mine.

The choice I did have was how I was going to deal with it, and that was what I couldn't figure out. It wasn't fair to ask Joey to wait around or eventually to move. But I also couldn't see myself letting her go.

I drove home, my heart in shreds.

"Hey Sammy." Joey was cocooned on the couch, Hank in her lap, when I walked in.

"Hey baby." I leaned over and kissed the top of her head, and Hank let out a little "rowr." I was going to miss him too, but I'd already decided that he and Joey would stay here. Even if I couldn't come home to them every day, I could imagine them both here, right where I'd left them, right where they belonged.

"How was the scrimmage?" she asked.

"Honestly? It was awful. And as soon as we finished, Coach called with the decision. Seattle. I have to be there at the end of next week."

"Hmm." Joey let out an almost disinterested little hum.

I sank onto the couch next to her and Hank leapt into my lap.

"Hey, you stole my cat," Joey laughed.

"He has free will," I told her. "He was my cat first."

As if to remind us that he was nobody's cat at all, Hank let out a low rumble and then moved up to the back of the couch. A moment later, his paws were in my hair, and Joey's hand was on my thigh.

"Seattle is nice."

"You've been there?"

"Seen pictures. Plus, you'll be an octopus."

"That's a good thing?" My tone was skeptical.

"Sure. Octopi are super smart and very crafty. Like you." Joey moved closer, leaning into me.

"You know everything's going to be okay, right?" she said, clinging to my side.

"No," I told her. "I don't know that. This changes... everything."

"But John..." she trailed off. "I just don't want you to think this changes anything. Not with us."

I looked deep into those brilliant blue eyes then, feeling exhausted by her optimism for the first time I could remember. "Joey," I told her. "This actually changes everything. There's no reason to pretend otherwise."

Her face fell when I said that and I immediately felt awful, like I'd kicked a kitten or something. But it didn't do me any good to have her refusing to accept the reality of the situation. It only made it harder for me. For both of us.

"You're not... you're not breaking up with me, right?" Joey's eyes were huge and there was an edge of panic in her voice.

The words were on the tip of my tongue. It made no sense to try to stay together when I was going to be living three thousand miles away. "We should," I said honestly, everything in me crumpling at the thought.

Joey was in my arms in the next second, pressed up against me, her chin tilted up. "I won't let you."

"You won't let me what?"

"I'm not going to let you break up with me."

Despite everything, I laughed. "I'm guessing you haven't been on the tail end of many breakups, but that's not really how it works."

She shook her head, her ponytail flying around and threatening to whack me in the face. Her arms wrapped my waist and she hung on like a sloth refusing to drop to the forest floor. "No."

"I'm not trying to do it at this moment," I assured her. "And it isn't like it's what I want. But I'm leaving in a month, and then we will literally never see each other. It's not fair to you."

"It is if I don't want anyone else. Ever." She squeezed me tighter.

"You can't say that now. Time will pass. You'll meet someone."

She pressed her head to my chest. "John?"

"Yeah." My words felt like they were coming out through sludge.

"Do me a favor?"

"Baby, I'll try." I felt incapable of pretty much anything.

"Stop talking. I'm fixing this."

Another laugh tried to come out at the thought that Joey believed she could singlehandedly stop the machine that was professional hockey just because she didn't like a decision. But I was too depressed and tired to laugh. Instead, I just held her another few moments, feeling my heart whispering goodbye even though she refused to hear it.

I breathed her warmth and optimism, wishing I could keep it close forever. I wasn't smart or crafty enough to figure out how, though.

I sighed. I was going to miss this. All of it.

CHAPTER 26

JOEY

DRAGONS WITH CREDENTIALS

I hated seeing John so defeated and I wished I could tell him what I had up my sleeve, but until I was sure it was going to work, I didn't want to make things worse. We spent the rest of the weekend at home, and the mood was dark. The only good thing was that Sunday morning, John called off the early trip to the gym, which meant we stayed in bed.

And while his energy for most things seemed depleted by the sadness surrounding his upcoming trade, he had plenty of energy in the bedroom. It might have been that sex was a release of some of the pent-up frustration I knew he felt around having decisions made about him that he couldn't control. If that was the case, I was all for this form of release. But I still missed my happy Sammy.

By Monday morning, it felt like he'd accepted the situation. He still wasn't happy about it, but at least he'd come to terms with it.

I, however, had not. And I was eager to finish up work Monday afternoon and get over to Clara and Sly's house. I told John I was having dinner with Elodie, just to allay any suspicions.

"Hey there," Clara said, greeting me at her front door. "Come on in."

I stepped through the door, and was immediately confronted with a tiny blond person dressed as a... dragon?

"Halt!" the tiny person screamed.

"Katie, that's not a very polite way to greet a guest," Clara told her.

The dragon guard ignored Clara and raised a sword, poking me in the chest with it.

"Katie!"

"State your name," Katie said.

I suppressed a laugh and tried to maintain the serious demeanor the interrogation seemed to demand. "Joey. Uh, Josephine Baxter."

"Which is it?" she demanded, the dragon snout slipping over her eyes before her non-sword wielding hand moved to push it back up. Clara let out an exasperated sigh and mouthed "sorry."

"Katie?" Sly's voice came from the back of the house. "Are you harassing the guests again?"

"Stand down, Silly. I'm making sure this stranger has the proper credentials," Katie called back.

"She's been watching a lot of movies with knights in them," Clara said.

I nodded, finding it hard to take the knight before me

seriously. Partially because she was adorable, and partially because she was dressed like a chubby baby dragon with a very rotund belly and giant green clawed feet.

"Now, state your business," Katie demanded, pointing her sword at me again.

"Dinner. And parade planning," I told her.

"At least I'm not the only one who got the third degree," another voice said, preceding a tall, pretty woman into the foyer. "I'm Hillary," she said, reaching out a hand for me to shake. She looked vaguely familiar, and I remembered John telling me that Mizzoni had married a singer.

"Joey," I told her, smiling past the sword in my chest.

"You said Josephine," the dragon reminded me.

"Joey is my nickname," I told them both.

"Well, come inside," Clara said, nudging the dragon out of the way. "We can finish the inspection with a drink in your hand at least."

As I followed the other women into the main part of the house, the dragon stepped close. "I like parades," she said. "Silly proposed to my mommy in a parade."

I hadn't heard that story, but it sounded like a good one. "Oh yeah?"

"Yep." The dragon leaned her sword against the couch and climbed up onto the cushions, making herself comfortable between two huge men I recognized from the pool bar. Simpson and Corny.

"Hi guys," I said, accepting the glass Sly pressed into my hand as he gave me a hug in greeting.

"Hey Joey," they both called.

"How's John doing with everything?" Clara asked, coming to lead me to another pair of chairs in the living room.

"I think he's moving into the acceptance phase."

"He better not be," Simpson grumbled. "This trade is not happening."

"We'll handle it," Corny told him, tilting his own beer back for a sip.

"Dinner will be in fifteen," Sly said, appearing from around the corner again with a pink apron tied around his waist. "Just getting the steak ready to grill."

"I don't like steak," Katie told him.

"Dragons eat hot dogs. We all know this," Sly said.

"Right." Katie grinned.

"Don't worry. I got you, Katie bear." The smile Sly gave Katie made a little piece of my heart fizz and pop. So stinking cute.

"So, I've got most of the parents and kids from the foundation set up," Corny said, leaning forward. "And the team, of course."

"And I've been through every business on Main Street," Clara told me. "There's a ton of support there. Most of them have been willing to help recruit others."

"That's amazing," I said, loving the way things were coming together.

Hillary reappeared from the kitchen, this time with a dark-haired man at her side who I recognized immediately as Stephano Mizzoni.

"Hello," he said, moving to shake my hand.

"Hi. I'm Joey."

"Stephano."

Clara had been positive that Mizzoni would want to be involved in any effort to keep John on the Wombats, and she also thought his support would carry some weight with the local bigwigs, since he'd been a foundation of the team in Wilcox.

"I've made some calls since I've been here and have a couple meetings this week," Stephano said. "The mayor is on our side, one hundred percent."

We talked some more about how the town was rallying around the idea of the parade and the effort to defeat the trade. But one question remained in my mind as I sat down to eat with John's loyal teammates.

"Do you really think that what the town has to say will matter?" I asked them. "The trade is about money, right?" I'd kept a brave face for John, but now I felt the reality of the situation weighing on me. If the trade went through, I could lose him.

"The town's support is really important," Mizzoni said. "And proving that John carries a ton of fan attention will make at least some difference."

"Plus the work he's done with his foundation," Corny pointed out. "If we can show management that this trade is a bad PR move, we might be able to reverse it."

"I wouldn't be helping if I didn't think there was a chance," Sly told us. "Rhino is stubborn, but he's also concerned with what's best for the team. And good PR is good for the team. Between Mizzoni's support and the town, we can probably at least get him to reconsider."

"And there's still time? Nothing's been signed?" Simpson

asked.

"Not until the end of this week," Sly said.

We spent the rest of the meal planning logistics, and by the time I left Clara and Sly's place, I felt certain we could stop the trade. The rest was up to John.

CHAPTER 27
JOHN

LIFE SUCKS. NOW, A PARADE!

Despite all the rushing around prior to the trade being finalized, there didn't seem to be a whole lot of urgency around the actual signing of the new contract or announcing things publicly.

"They're gonna wait until after this parade, I'm sure," my agent told me.

"I'm not even sure I should participate," I said, doing my best to keep up my positivity but failing, as had been the norm for the past week. I felt bad for Joey, who had been like a bluebird trying to keep flying cheerfully along despite a tornado whirling around her. "I'm not going to be part of the team much longer."

"You're on the team until you're officially not on the team," Shotz said. He wasn't exactly Shakespeare, but he was a good agent. "And leaving the team is going to double your take home in this particular situation. Don't forget that."

"I'd give it up to stay."

"I know. But you'll see in time—this is a great deal."

"Right." It was. And a year ago I might have been thrilled with it. But I suspected that even without Joey's reappearance in my life and Mizzoni's sudden departure, I'd be less than eager to start again somewhere new. I was happy here. I'd felt at home here. I'd actually believed this was a home for me—between the Foundation and Joey... well, there was no point dwelling on it now.

"Come on, you're going to be late," Joey said, appearing from the bedroom. She wore slim jeans and a tank top that showed off her fit shoulders, and I was tempted to push her right back into the bedroom. We'd spent a lot of time in there this week. It was the only thing that distracted me from my reality.

"I don't think it would matter a whole lot if I was late," I told her.

"It would. Trust me." Joey flashed a smile that would have had me suspicious if I wasn't in the process of snagging her hand and pulling her into my chest. "John," she growled, but her resistance turned into a laugh and then she tilted her chin up and I dropped my mouth to hers.

Sunshine and laughter filled me when we kissed, all the promise of a future we might still share. I was doing my best to believe we could really have it all, but even when Joey was in my arms it still felt like she was slipping from my grasp.

"Let's go," she said, breaking away and pulling on my hand. I was wearing a jersey, as directed, and it was heavy on my shoulders. Like a mantle I no longer deserved. The glow and promise of the woman I loved faded, the farther she moved away from me. What would life be like in Seattle?

Lonely.

Dark.

Full of cloudy skies and rain showers.

"Yep. Let's get this over with," I agreed, trying to make my tone upbeat even if my words were anything but.

As we headed to the arena, I watched my town go by through the windshield. Every little thing in Wilcox had taken on a nostalgic tint, as if I was seeing the whole world through a sepia filter. The back streets of my green little neighborhood, the way the rink pushed up against the bright blue sky like a fortress. I would miss it. All of it.

"There you are," Sly boomed as Joey and I stepped down from the truck.

I checked my watch. "Dude, we're not late."

"Didn't say you were," Sly told me with a grin, and then he gave a nod over my shoulder to Solamentes and Simpson, who headed inside the rink.

A huge flatbed with rails was hitched to the team truck, and Julius Ramon waved from behind the wheel. There were at least ten other cars lined up behind the truck, all decorated with Wombat colors and some sporting our stuffed mascot tied to their antennas, it's blue jersey and tiny pink helmet vibrant in the sun.

"We're riding up here," Simpson told me, pointing up to the platform. "So we can wave at our admirers and whatnot."

"Whatnot," I agreed.

The trailer seemed like a fundamentally bad idea, unless

the hope was to kill us all in one fell swoop if something were to happen. But the other guys were all leaping up and leaning down to give a hand to the rest of us, so I just followed suit.

"I can see the headline now. Pro Hockey Team Dies in Parade," I muttered.

"Dude, this thing is gonna be going like ten miles an hour, tops." Corny chucked me on the shoulder. "I'm getting tired of this whole Eeyore thing you've got going on, Samuels."

"Yeah? You're tired of it?" I asked him. "How do you think I feel?" I sounded like a whiny little girl. No, strike that, even Clara's kid Katie was more put together and mature than I sounded at that moment. But I didn't care. My defenses were crumbling. This stupid, ridiculous parade was going to be the very last time I'd be a Wombat in public, and if I didn't keep myself surly and mad, I'd break down in tears.

"Get a grip," Sly said, climbing up beside me.

"I'm trying," I told him. He dropped a reassuring hand on my shoulder and gave it a squeeze.

"It'll all work out," he said.

"One way or another," I muttered.

The team loaded up, each of us leaning over the rickety sidewalls of the flatbed as the truck began to move smoothly forward. Julius Ramon was proving that his driving skills extended beyond ice cleaning machines, and I settled a bit.

The parking lot, which had been filled with wives, girlfriends, and a few fans, emptied out as everyone climbed into Wombat-themed vehicles to follow the parade route. I did a double take as I thought I spotted Mizzoni and his fiancée Hillary climbing into my truck with Joey. But that didn't make sense. He wouldn't come back for a measly local parade.

"Hey," I asked Sly. "Is Mizzoni in town?"

Sly looked my way to answer, but the motion of the truck distracted him.

We pulled out of the rink parking lot and cruised slowly a block or two before turning onto Main Street, and when the truck straightened out, moving along the wide-open thoroughfare, I had to blink hard to be sure I wasn't hallucinating.

The sidewalks were packed with people, and lights had been strung from one side of the street to the other. Wombats signs hung from buildings, sporting slogans like, "Wombat Dominance!" and "The Furriest Force on Ice! Go Wombats!"

The general support that had turned out for an informal parade celebrating nothing was shocking, but the real surprise were the other signs I spotted—the ones held up like picket signs in a protest.

Samuels Stays!

Keep Our Goalie at Home!

John Samuels is Our Man!

No Trade!

If He Goes, We Don't Come!

"What the fuck?" I asked the truck at large.

Sly and Simpson hooted at my side and Solamentes slid over to slap my back. "Town doesn't want you to go, man."

The noise from the crowd was unbelievable, but not as hard to accept as the fact that every single sign I spotted had my name on it.

"What is this?" I asked the chaos around me.

"It's a protest," Rock Stevens said.

"For me?"

"Yeah, for you. We're not letting you be traded without weighing in on the matter, and we thought the fans might have a few thoughts."

I stared out over the crowd unable to process what I was seeing. The people were stacked four and five deep on the sidewalk, screaming my name and calling out their support.

When the flatbed came to a stop at the end of the main drag, I expected that we'd turn and head back to the arena, but Ramon pulled us up sideways instead, next to a makeshift stage.

There were chairs and a podium, and as the engine shut off and the crowd began to quiet, the mayor stepped up to the microphone.

"Welcome Wilcox!" he called out, causing the crowd to erupt in screams once again. When they quieted down, he went on. "Thanks for coming out today to show your love and support for our professional hockey team." He grinned at us.

"You know, a town of this size generally doesn't rate a pro sports team, but Wilcox is special, and so are the Wombats."

He paused while the crowd exploded again.

"And today, we're here specifically to press the case for

one of our own. As you may know, the team is considering a trade. Our brand new starting goalie, youngest in the league, is being sent off to play for another team. What do you think about that?"

The crowd erupted in jeers and boos, and a little glimmer of happiness lit inside me. At least they'd miss me, I guessed. Punches and slaps came from my teammates, and a warm blush climbed my cheeks.

"The thing is," the mayor went on. "No one asked us, did they?"

"No!" The crowd called back.

"And I, for one, am not ready to let John Samuels go without an argument."

"Woot!" Sly called out.

"So today, we're here to make a case in hopes that the team's management might take notice. We'd like to keep our rookie right where he is. Here are a few reasons why."

As the mayor stepped back, a line of kids filed onto the stage one by one, and I recognized them from camp. Each little face turned my way, and a few hands raised. I waved back, emotion swelling inside me as James, one of the dads I met last week, took the microphone from the mayor.

"I have something to say," James said, looking uncertainly out at the crowd. He caught my eye, and a smile lit his face as he turned back to the gathered masses. "I don't know John Samuels personally. I met him last week for the first time, but I knew him as a member of this team and respected his talent. Especially the way he stepped up when Mizzoni got injured."

There were scattered cheers from the crowd.

"And I know the trade is about him as a player, about his talent. But I also know that we need good men like Samuels here in Wilcox. My son attended Futures on Ice last week. And I am not exaggerating when I tell you that it changed his life." James looked around as if expecting to be interrupted, but then continued, dropping one hand to the shoulder of his son, who I remembered well. Adam.

"My kid was struggling a little. I can admit that, as a family, we were struggling. My wife died this year and it's been hard. For both of us. But I watched my kid bend and I've been worried he might break. Hockey is his favorite sport, so when I found out about the camp, I looked into it. But money's tight, so I didn't mention it to him. The thing is, John Samuels called me personally to assure me that he'd find a spot for us and that he'd get it covered financially." James looked back at his kid.

"And that camp? Yeah, maybe it's just a game... " his voice cracked. "But it gave us both something new, something to be excited about, something to look forward to..."

Adam was a good player. But more than that, I saw what his father was talking about. He'd started the week quiet and withdrawn, but ended it with a smile and a promise to keep practicing. I knew we'd made a difference for him. I was proud of it.

"He's the kind of man this town can't afford to lose."

Cheers went up from the crowd and I was horrified to feel a lump in my throat. I swallowed it down as my eyes swung away from the stage, but my gaze locked with one man standing just below the truck platform where I stood. The steely eyes were narrowed and surrounded by a host of crow's feet that I didn't remember being there. They widened when our focus met, and the breath pushed out of me.

Dad.

"You okay, dude?" Solamentes pounded my back as if I'd been choking.

I glanced at him. "Yeah, fine." I turned back to my father.

There was too much noise and chaos around us to say anything to him, and I wasn't quite sure what I'd say anyway. But just as I lifted a hand in acknowledgement, another person strode confidently onto the stage in front of the crowd, and the noise level rose again.

Mizzoni. "Hello Wilcox," he said, his voice smooth and strong, just as I remembered it from the locker room chats we'd had when I'd first joined the team. "Man, I've missed this place." The crowd cheered.

"When I left, though, I did it with a clear mind because I knew the team, and my position were in good hands. John's hands."

More noise erupted.

This entire situation was surreal. What town got involved in the inner workings of their pro sports team's management decisions? What town essentially attempted a coup? This was insane.

Mizzoni talked for a little while, and I found his girlfriend Hillary in the crowd, near the stage. Standing next to the woman I could pick out of any crowd, any time. Joey. Just as I found her, she turned and shot a wide, glittering smile at me that pulled a reaction from every bit and bob inside my body. She was like a fucking magnet.

I shook my head at her, trying to communicate my complete sense of overwhelm, but her smile never wavered. In fact, it grew so wide I began to wonder if she didn't have something to do with all this.

Mizzoni wrapped up his speech by calling the team management to the stage, and I watched in shock as Slater, the team's manager made his way through the crowd. My stomach clenched—there was a good chance he wasn't going to be especially pleased about being second guessed this way... but as he took the microphone from Mizzoni, Rhino shot me a half smile and ran a hand across his short hair as he stood next to Slater.

"You know," Slater began. "My job as this team's manager is to make smart decisions that give us the best odds of bringing a cup home to Wilcox. And that's what this trade was about. Or that was how it began, at least." He looked over the crowd, which had fallen almost silent.

"But part of what makes a team successful in a small town like Wilcox is the support of the fans. And the fact that all of you were willing to come out this evening to show your support for a player, to express your desire to keep him here... well, I don't take that lightly."

The crowd gave a little cheer, but like them, I realized he hadn't made any commitments.

"The thing is, this is a business decision," he went on, eliciting a few boos from the crowd. "And I'm not the only one involved. However," he said, waving a hand to try to quiet those beginning to jeer. "I will take your opinions into account. We need the town's support to continue to operate here, and you've made your opinion in this matter very clear. I will see what I can do about keeping John Samuels on the roster," Slater said.

"As a starter!" someone yelled loudly, and I looked down in shock, realizing it was my father.

"Yeah!" someone else followed.

Soon, the whole crowd was screaming again, and the cacophony evolved into a chant that blew my mind. "Samuels! Samuels! Samuels!"

These things were not decided by crowds of people at impromptu parades—I knew that and so did they. But it was incredible to see the support the town was willing to offer their team. To offer me. And as the sheer shock of the entire thing rolled through me, I met my father's eyes again, and my knees nearly went out.

When had Dad ever plead my case? When had he ever taken the time to stand up for me, to support me?

It was all too much, and when the truck rumbled to life again, as the crowd cheered and screamed my name, exhaustion pushed through me like a herd of wild horses.

The last few weeks of uncertainty, and now this? I needed a very long nap.

No, I thought again. What I needed was Joey.

CHAPTER 28

JOEY

THE RING THING

Clara and I were gripping each other's hands with excitement as we watched the town of Wilcox turn out en masse to support keeping John on the team. Hearing the cheers and shouts, and seeing his teammates and fans step up for the man I loved made me irrationally happy.

"If this doesn't do it, Rhino has a heart of stone," Clara told me as we rode back to the parking lot at the arena through the dissipating crowd on Main Street.

"He doesn't," Sly put in. "He's a businessman, sure—maybe the trade made good financial sense, but part of business is keeping tabs on your image. And trading a hometown favorite? Not a good look."

"Have you mentioned anything to him?" I asked. "I know it must be a hard spot for you to be in—kinda in the middle?"

"Nah. I'm still a player first. He doesn't put much stock in what I tell him. But I definitely voiced my opinion on this one. And suggested he clear up his schedule to attend this parade tonight."

Clara peered around at the scattered faces outside. "Oh, yeah. Was he there?"

"I don't know what the guy looks like," I said, feeling unhelpful.

"He was there. I saw him over by the podium toward the end," Sly said. "He looked a little miffed while Slater talked."

"Oh well," I sang, glee doing a little jig inside me. I couldn't wait to see John, to take in his shock and surprise.

I didn't have to wait long. He was standing in the center of the parking lot as we pulled in, his strong arms crossed over his chest as he watched Sly navigate the truck into a spot. I slid out and skipped over to him. "Oh my gosh," I gushed. "That was incredible."

His expression was hard to read. He looked almost...angry? "I don't even know what to say," he said. "That was bizarre."

"But good, right?" I needed to touch him, and I reached out and laid a hand over his forearm, feeling him relax under my fingers.

"I guess? Really unexpected."

I nodded, bouncing on my toes. "Think it'll work?" I asked.

"Joey," he said, watching my face intently. "Did you have anything to do with all this?"

I glanced around innocently. "What, this?"

"Yeah," he said, his full lips stretching into a little smile. "This." He tugged me up against his chest.

"I don't know what you mean," I said, batting my lashes up at him.

"Did you call my dad?" he asked.

"I might have had a chat with your brother..."

"And the mayor?"

"Don't be silly. I just moved here. I don't know the mayor personally." I smiled up at him, still playing innocent.

"But Clara does."

"She might," I admitted.

"I can't believe you did this," he said, his voice dropping to a whisper. "For me."

"For you," I agreed. "I think I'd do anything for you, Sammy. You don't know that by now?"

John's smile lit the entire parking lot, lifting everything inside me and draping it with radiance and sunshine.

"There you are." Mr. Samuels had a booming voice with an edge of sandpaper. It had frightened me a bit in high school, and it hadn't softened with age.

"Dad, hi." John released me and turned to greet his father. "Teej!"

John's brother stepped forward and pulled him into a huge hug. "Hey squeak. Hi Joey. Good to see you again." TJ leaned in and kissed my cheek.

"Thanks for coming," I told them both.

"It was quite a turnout," TJ said. "This town's got your back, baby bro."

John stood speechless, looking between his father, his brother, and me with a mystified expression on his face. I was about to suggest we go out for a bite or something, partially to relieve the awkward tension that had settled around us, but there was no need. Half the team descended on John, manhandling him with awkward man hugs and socking him on the shoulders.

"There's the golden boy," Rock declared. "Oh hey, you've got a better-looking twin."

"Meet my brother TJ," John said to the noisy group. "And my dad, Earl."

"You all must be pretty impressed with this guy," Sly suggested to them both.

"We are," TJ said.

Mr. Samuels was wide eyed and silent, regarding the group of enormous, noisy men with what looked like suspicion and awe mixed up in a questionable cocktail.

"Anyone up for a little visit to Paddy's?" Corny asked the group. "Celebrate the very likely reality that we're keeping our goalie?"

"Might be premature," John said. "I don't want to jinx anything."

"So superstitious," Rock told him, tousling his hair. "Come on, a couple beers with your boys and your old man won't change anything."

"Let's do that," Earl said, coming out of his catatonic state. "Son, let's go have a beer."

John just nodded back at everyone, and took my hand, as if for security. I gave his warm fingers a squeeze, and then turned to TJ and Earl. "We can all fit in John's truck."

Fifteen minutes later, we were all around the pool table in the back of Paddy's, and I sat at a little high-top table with John, TJ, and Mr. Samuels, whose eyes kept finding the ring on my finger and resting there. He didn't say anything, and I wasn't sure it was my place to mention it, so I just stayed close to John and followed his lead.

It was clear how uncomfortable things were between John and his dad, but TJ was a good buffer, talking to each of them and pretending not to notice that they barely spoke to each other.

"So, when will the wedding be?" TJ asked us.

John and I exchanged a look. "We were waiting to see how this trade panned out," John said after a moment.

"Ah, yeah. Makes sense," TJ said.

"But what about you?" I asked him. "You're engaged, aren't you?"

TJ grinned widely, and the look was so happy my heart melted a little for how clearly he loved his fiancée. "Yeah," he said. "Next summer."

"No rush when it's real," Mr. Samuels shot out, sounding grumpy despite the beer in front of him.

"Right," I agreed. "And will you get married back in Peach Tree Grove?" I asked. I wondered if they'd have the reception at the General E. Lee. Or use the same caterer I'd booked.

"Tabitha is from Atlanta," TJ said. "So she's got her heart set on a wedding there."

"Of course," I said.

"And you guys? Will you come home for the wedding?" TJ asked us.

John and I exchanged a look. We hadn't discussed any of this yet. The engagement wasn't fake after all—but in some ways it still didn't feel quite real.

"We haven't gotten to the details yet," John said.

"Sir," I said to Mr. Samuels, my heart stuttering when he turned cold eyes upon me. I swallowed, steeling my spine. "I just wanted to say thank you. I know this was the boys' mother's ring, and I know that makes it really special. It means more than anything to me that John proposed with it, and it's really the most beautiful thing I could ever have imagined." I paused, swallowing again. "But I wanted to tell you that I'm happy to give it back to you if it's too hard. Seeing it. On me, I mean."

Mr. Samuels stared at the ring on my hand, glinting merrily beneath the dim overhead lights in the bar. For a long moment his eyes stuck there, and I felt John tense at my side. But then Mr. Samuels reached a hand out to me, and I dropped the hand with the ring into his, feeling the weathered skin of his palm as he looked up to meet my gaze. His eyes were shining and his expression had softened.

"I think Marianne's ring looks beautiful on you, Josephine. And I think she would be pleased to know you are wearing it."

I smiled at him, my skin warming at the thought that John's mother would be happy to see me wearing her ring. I turned to glance at John, but his eyes were on the tabletop, and my attention was pulled back to Mr. Samuels as he said something else, in a much quieter voice.

"You know, she was so excited about having a second kid. And the last thing she said to me, when she held little John there in her arms, was that she'd be looking after him from beyond." He sniffed, and I felt tears building in my throat as I reached for John's thigh under the table at my side.

Mr. Samuels went on. "Sometimes I think she might be disappointed with me, actually. I was the one who was here, and I didn't do such a good job looking after him."

John was quiet, and I knew why. Mr. Samuels hadn't been a great father. He hadn't been a good one, either. But it was hard to look at the man at my side, so full of pain and regret, and hold onto anger.

"You were grieving, Dad." John said it quietly.

"Doesn't make it right." Mr. Samuels picked up his beer and finished it. Then he looked between his boys and said, "I'm just glad you boys stayed close." And then he stood and headed off to the bar.

It was almost as if a shroud had been lifted from our table and now the party going on around us picked up volume again.

"Well," TJ said, laughing uncomfortably.

"Yeah," John said.

"That was a long time coming, I guess," TJ said.

John shrugged, took a drink and then said, "Actually never thought I'd hear that. It wasn't a 'sorry,' of course..."

"Close enough?" TJ asked.

John sighed. "Yeah." His tone was tired, as if it would be easier to just dismiss the topic than argue for the words he really deserved. "Hang on," he said, pulling his phone out of his pocket and looking at it. "It's Shotz," he told me, standing and moving away from the table to answer the call.

"His agent," I told TJ.

Rock Stevens had been standing nearby and he turned when I said this. "Shotz called?"

"He's talking to him right now," I told him.

Rock alerted a few of the other guys, and by the time John returned to the table, the team was assembled and waiting, staring at him.

"Well?" Sly asked him.

John's face broke into a wide smile, and he let out a light laugh, shaking his head. "I can't really believe it, but that little parade did the trick. I'm staying!"

The entire bar erupted in shouts and cheers, and as I glanced toward the bar, where Mr. Samuels sat with his beer, watching, he raised his glass toward the celebration around his younger son.

"Sammy!" I shouted, throwing myself into John's arms when his teammates had finished congratulating him. "I'm so happy!"

"Me too," he said, nuzzling his mouth down against my neck. "God, I thought I was gonna lose you."

"You going to Seattle would not have meant you losing me," I told him, pressing myself against him and feeling my blood heat. "I'd never let you get away."

"Well this makes everything much easier," he said, pulling back and then dropping his mouth to mine.

He kissed me sweet and soft, his hands on my waist pulling me close, and I sighed into his mouth, not even real- izing just how worried I'd really been. He was staying here. We were staying together.

"Marry me," he whispered in my ear.

"I already said yes," I reminded him with a giggle.

"I know, but let's not wait. Let's get married now."

"Now?" I stepped back, needing to see his expression, which was earnest and sweet. "Like tonight?"

"Not tonight, but... tomorrow?"

My mind spun. I wanted to, but my parents would certainly have simultaneous heart attacks. "What if we get married twice?" I asked him quietly.

"Not following."

"Once just for us. And once for everyone else."

He grinned. "I like it." He kissed me again, and then got tugged away to the bar for a round of shots with the team to celebrate. I watched him with his teammates, his friends, my body so full of warmth and happiness I didn't want the moment to end.

"He loves you," TJ said, leaning over my shoulder. "He always has."

I turned around and hugged TJ, mostly to expel a tiny bit of the energy that was building inside me, making me feel like I'd burst. "It's mutual," I told him. "And it always has been."

CHAPTER 29
JOHN

THE PAST IS THE FUTURE

TJ and Dad stayed the weekend, TJ crashing on the couch and Dad taking the guest room that had once been Joey's. Over the course of those days, Dad relaxed, letting the years of distrust and hurt slide off into a pile we both managed to sweep away with new memories and conversations years in the making.

"Your mother was one hundred percent sure you'd be a girl," Dad told me as we sat around the kitchen table over steaks the last night they were in town.

"Really?" I asked, happy to hear any details about my mother and what she might have thought about me, the son she never really knew. "So she was disappointed?"

Dad chuckled, his eyes taking on the faraway look he'd worn a lot this weekend—whenever he'd talked about Mama. "Not even a little bit," he said.

I sat with that for a moment, wondering if he was just saying that to make me feel better. But I didn't think that was in his skill set, actually.

"She was with you about twenty-four hours, you know," Dad went on as Joey held my hand under the table, steady and strong at my side just like she'd been all weekend. "She held you almost that entire time. Didn't want to let you go, even when the alarms were all blaring, and the doctors were racing around trying to save her." He shook his head sadly.

"Her mother brought TJ to the hospital to meet you right after you were born, do you remember Teej?"

My brother shook his head, a faraway smile on his face. "I was too young to remember."

"Well I remember," Dad said softly. "And she looked at the two of you together, and she was so happy. So wildly happy." A tear dripped down my father's rough skin and I looked away, a misplaced embarrassment rising inside me. This man didn't cry. He didn't even feel, as far as I was aware.

"She said it was the best thing, having two boys. She knew she wasn't gonna be there... " Dad trailed off and sniffed. "And she said you'd look after each other, that brothers were the best thing we could have made."

Dad stared at his plate for a long moment, his shoulders shaking slightly, as TJ and I sat immobilized. This was a version of Dad neither of us knew how to react to.

"You all miss her," Joey said softly. "She sounds like a wonderful mother. I wish I could have met her."

Dad nodded and I pushed down the emotion threatening to rush up my throat, looking up to catch TJ wiping at his eyes before picking up his knife to cut a bite of steak.

"She would have been proud. Of both of you," Dad said, looking between TJ and me. "And so am I."

It was by far the most I'd ever gotten from Dad, and I took his words and folded them up neatly to store for later. They'd be something I took out now and then to look at, to remember this moment. It was still surreal to have heard them spoken aloud.

Anyone could change and grow, I realized, given the right circumstances.

My eyes drifted to Joey, and I found it was almost hard to look right at her, she was so brilliantly perfect. The girl I'd loved my whole life, who would be by my side as we discovered our next chapters together. She'd grown and shifted before my eyes too, and I hoped I could do the same, growing into the man she deserved, and the goalie the Wombats needed.

I squeezed her hand and met her eyes, my whole future lighting up inside her gaze.

CHAPTER 30

JOEY

THE GLASS BANANA

True to his word, John Samuels married me the next day. We dropped his father and brother at the airport, and drove straight to the county offices to fill out paperwork and say our vows in front of a judge.

Our witness was a woman named Marge, who wore an eyepatch and a brightly colored dress with feathers in her hair, and the man reciting our vows was certainly not going to win awards for being passionate about his job.

But none of it mattered. The only people I was really aware of in that little room were me and John.

He stood in front of me, holding both my hands in his, and his warm smile penetrated every cell in my body.

"I, John Martin Samuels, take you, Josephine Adelaide Baxter, to be my lawfully wedded wife."

Wife... the word wove through me and left a trail of sparkly joy behind it. I smiled back at him and said the same words to him. "I, Josephine Adelaide Baxter, take you,

John Martin Samuels, to be my lawfully wedded husband..." And the word husband left a twin trail inside my heart as John's dark eyes filled with emotion.

"Not everyone does it, but if you want, you can kiss now," the officiant told us.

John grinned and stepped close, wrapping a hand around my waist and cupping my cheek with his other. "Oh, I'm gonna kiss her," he told the man. "Stand back."

The officiant actually did take a step back, and John's lips met mine with an explosion—or maybe that was only in my head. Warmth and joy flooded my body at the contact, every living part of me celebrating the total rightness of the moment, of the future we were planning together.

The kiss went on for a while—I wasn't timing it, but the officiant did clear his throat at one point to try to break it up. But John took his time, his tongue meeting mine and flushing my body hot with desire as my arms wrapped his strong back, holding on for all I was worth.

When he finally set me upright again, my head spun, and I flashed a smile at the officiant. "Thanks," I told him.

"You should be thanking him," the guy said, pointing at John. "That was some kiss."

"Thanks," I whispered to John, laughing. "For loving me."

"Any time," John said back. "And forever."

We held hands as we left the courthouse, the smile on my face so wide it felt permanent. I couldn't imagine ever being unhappy again—with John at my side and our life stretching out before us laden with promise and possibility...

"What about the honeymoon?" John asked, stopping me on the steps of the courthouse.

"What?"

"Do we do it now or after the next wedding?"

I thought about that for a brief moment. "Um, both?"

John grinned. "Good plan."

It was still off season for hockey, but all of this happened so fast, and I knew John was still hoping to make All Star this year to cement his spot. "You probably don't have time for a trip though, do you?"

"I'll make time," he said. "Where should we go?"

Ideas rushed through me, but I found I didn't care at all, as long as we were together. "Clara told me the team is headed to Deck Gillespie's lake house next weekend..." I tried to imagine honeymooning with a hockey team. John's face said he couldn't picture it either.

"Not sure about that... but I could get into you and me, alone in a cabin on the lake..."

"Ohh, yes," I agreed. "Maybe we go a bit early and catch up with them when they all arrive?"

"Plan," he agreed.

Two days later, we were ensconced in a little A-frame cabin on the edge of a Virginia lake, Gillespie's massive lake house directly across from us. The team wouldn't arrive for several more days, and we planned to make the most of our accommodation, which was mostly just a king-sized bed, a tiny kitchen, and an enormous deck on the waterfront.

"It's not quite the lap of luxury," John had said when we arrived and unlocked the door. In his voice I heard the tone I recognized from high school, from before high school. The one that apologized for coming from a family that didn't use a finger bowl at place settings and didn't consider cotillion as fundamental as getting one's teeth cleaned.

I dropped my bag and turned to him, feeling every bit of the glorious isolation and beauty that our setting provided. "Mr. Samuels."

John's grin crept slowly across his face as my hands rested on his chest. He turned to face me fully. "Yes, Mrs. Samuels?"

"This is the single best vacation I've ever been on. We have absolutely everything we will ever need right here." I pressed myself into him. "You, Sammy. You are everything I'll ever need."

His arms enclosed me, and we stood there for a moment, drinking in the cool lakeside air, the silence of the woods around the cabin. John's body was warm and hard against me—hard in one spot especially.

"Mr. Samuels?"

"Yes, Mrs. Samuels?"

"Did you bring a pepper grinder in your pocket?"

"What?" John laughed but didn't let me go.

"Or is it maybe a candlestick?"

"It is not."

"Glass banana?"

"While I often carry a glass banana, I left it home for our honeymoon."

"Hmm," I said, letting my hand slip lower to press against the front of John's pants. "Mind if I investigate?"

John walked us backward to the bed against the back wall. "I wish you would," he said, his voice dropping low.

I let my hands move to his waistband, unbuttoning his jeans and then pressing them down, along with his boxers.

"So not a banana, then," I said, giggling. I let my hand slide over John's very impressive not-banana, and he hissed out a sharp breath.

"Have I mentioned how much I like it when you wear sundresses?" he whispered, tugging me down onto the mattress.

"No," I said, playing along and climbing to sit astride him as he pulled off his T-shirt. I pressed myself along the hard ridge of his erection, loving the heat and pressure exactly where I wanted it. John's voice rumbled in his chest as his hands found my waist. "I really, really like it."

"Why would that be?" I asked, letting him control the motion as I slid up and down along his length.

He dropped one hand, rubbing me through the thin fabric of my panties before pushing them to the side and notching himself to enter. "This," he hissed, guiding me onto him. "Because of this..."

I let my head drop back as he filled me completely, enjoying the sensation of being utterly and totally full, impaled on him in the best way.

We moved together, the lake as our backdrop and the distant call of birds the only soundtrack besides our own labored breathing. Soon, I felt sensation building toward a climax, my nerves tingling and my legs beginning to shake as my rhythm broke down.

"I need..."

But I didn't have to tell him. John knew exactly what I needed—he always had. And when we finished, I collapsed to his side, curled in the nook of his arm, my hand resting on his solid chest and loving the feel of him breathing beneath it.

"What do you need?" he asked softly, picking up where I'd left off when my orgasm had overtaken me.

"Only this. Just you. Us," I told him, sleepy.

"You've got it. For as long as you want."

"Just forever," I said.

We had four days like that—and on the fifth day, a speedboat careened across the lake carrying a crowd of noisy men, and we joined them, celebrating life and love and hockey ahead of the start of the new season.

EPILOGUE

JULIUS RAMON

The town had spoken, and the Wombats were keeping John. It was a truth that made my heart warm, since I admired him greatly. He was not Stephano. And that was to his benefit. Each player is different. Each player has strengths and weaknesses that combine to make him unique. And John has many strengths that will serve the Wombats well, and he's a fan favorite. When the All Star announcements came out, guess who was selected?

The funny thing is, John elected not to play on the advice of Rhino and Shotz, who needed him to focus on the coming season instead. They couldn't have their starting goalie hurt just before his first full season.

Want more Wombats?

Be sure to join Delancey's Fancies here so you'll have the very latest information when the next book comes out! Get early releases, sneak peeks and freebies! (And a weekly photo of my loyal lab, Charlie Taco!)

ALSO BY DELANCEY STEWART

Want more? Get early releases, sneak peeks and freebies! Join my mailing list here or scan the QR code and get a free story!

The Wilcox Wombats Series:

Checking the Center

The Wedding Winger

Grumpy Goalie

Puck Proposal

The Kasper Ridge Series:

Only a Summer

Only a Fling

Only a Crush

Only a Secret

Only a Touch

The Singletree Series:

Happily Ever His

Happily Ever Hers

Shaking the Sleigh

Second Chance Spring

Falling Into Forever

Singletree Box Set 1

Singletree Box Set 2

The Digital Dating Series (with Marika Ray):

Texting with the Enemy

While You Were Texting

Save the Last Text

How to Lose a Girl in 10 Texts

The Text Before Christmas

The MR. MATCH Series:

Prequel: Scoring a Soulmate

Book One: Scoring the Keeper's Sister

Book Two: Scoring a Fake Fiancée

Book Three: Scoring a Prince

Book Four: Scoring with the Boss

Book Five: Scoring a Holiday Match

Mr. Match: The Boxed Set

The KINGS GROVE Series:

When We Let Go

Open Your Eyes

When We Fall

Open Your Heart

Christmas in Kings Grove

The STARR RANCH WINERY Series:

Chasing a Starr

THE GIRLFRIENDS OF GOTHAM Series:

Men and Martinis

Highballs in the Hamptons

Cosmos and Commitment

The Girlfriends of Gotham Box Set

STANDALONES:

Let it Snow

Without Words

Without Promises

Mr. Big

Adagio

The PROHIBITED! Duet:

Prohibited!

The Glittering Life of Evie Mckenzie